ALEXANDER McCALL SMITH

THE EXQUISITE ART

of

GETTING EVEN

First published in hardback in Great Britain in 2022 by Polygon,
an imprint of Birlinn Ltd. This paperback edition published
in Great Britain in 2023 by Polygon.

Birlinn Ltd
West Newington House
10 Newington Road
Edinburgh
EH9 1QS

9 8 7 6 5 4 3 2 1

www.polygonbooks.co.uk

ISBN 978 1 84697 642 1
EBOOK ISBN 978 1 78885 564 8

British Library Cataloguing-in-Publication Data
A catalogue record for this book is available on
request from the British Library.

Typeset in Sabon and Adobe Garamond by The Foundry, Edinburgh
Printed and bound in Great Britain by Clays Ltd, Elcograf S.p.A.

THE EXQUISITE ART

of

GETTING EVEN

ALEXANDER McCALL SMITH is one of the world's most prolific and most popular authors. His various series of books have been translated into over forty-six languages and have sold more than thirty million copies across the world. These include the *No. 1 Ladies' Detective Agency* series, the *44 Scotland Street* novels, the Isabel Dalhousie novels and the von Igelfeld series. He also writes stand-alone novels, poetry, children's fiction, and libretti for short operas.

CONTENTS

This book is for Graham Weir

SWEET VENGEANCE

An Introduction

A desire for revenge is something that every one of us must have felt at one time or another, unless, of course, we are saints – which most of us are not. Somebody wrongs us and, as we nurse our pain and sense of injustice, we imagine the wrongdoer having exactly the same thing done to him or her – or even worse. This is revenge: the biter bit, and it is very satisfactory, a great theme for Elizabethan drama.

Why – and whether – we should feel that way about revenge is a question that has interested students of human nature as much as it has troubled philosophers. The impulse to exact revenge is undoubtedly strong in the human psyche: one only has to observe the behaviour of small children to see how it rears its head at a very early stage. As W.H. Auden observed in his much appreciated (although subsequently suppressed) poem "September 1, 1939": *I and the public know / What all schoolchildren learn / Those to whom evil is done / Do evil in return.* Auden was talking about political pathology, based on international wrongs, but the same observation might be made about our ordinary quotidian experience.

Where does this desire for revenge come from? At

its heart, there seems to be some notion of justice and reciprocity. What you do to others, you must expect to be done to you – that seems only fair. If we are to live together in harmony, it might be argued, it is important that the scales be balanced – everyone must understand that those who seek an unfair advantage over others will pay for what they do.

But, strictly speaking, that is not so much revenge as retribution. Revenge is more personal – it is an action performed with a view to satisfying the feelings of one who has been wronged. Revenge has nothing to do with ensuring social peace or correcting any imbalance. It is invoked purely to make the wronged person feel better. Revenge is quite different from dispassionate retribution or correction: it is for this reason that revenge has been described as "wild justice".

Of course, that does not make revenge morally right. In fact, seeking revenge has always made philosophers feel uncomfortable. Exacting revenge adds to the sum total of human suffering, rather than subtracts from it. And, in terms of the recovery of the victim, there is a lot to be said for showing mercy and forgiveness rather than insisting on revenge. Forgiveness is more healing than the infliction of pain: there is ample evidence for that proposition, as any study of conflict resolution will tend to confirm. You don't necessarily get better by making another suffer.

And yet, we remain fascinated by revenge, which still plays a part in our affairs no matter how hard we try to overcome the urge to get even. We should not delude ourselves, though, as to the sterility of revenge. No Sicilian or Appalachian blood feud was ever ended by the taking of revenge, and we would do well to remind ourselves of that. Having said that, I am reminded of the story of the Spanish conquistador who, on his death bed, is asked by his confessor whether he has forgiven his enemies. "Enemies?" he replies. "I have no enemies, Father. I have killed them all."

The four stories that follow are all tales of revenge. Each has a particular background in terms of something that I have experienced or thought about. The first story, "Vengeance Is Mine", occurred to me after I had paid a visit to a small Caribbean island some years ago. There was only one town of any consequence on this island, and that was more of a village than a town. Yet, as I walked down the main street there, a very large and extremely ostentatious car made its way down the road. I saw that the driver was a comparatively young man. Now, there are various ways of acquiring such a car, some of them even honest. I had the distinct impression that this car, though, might have been the fruit of less than honest activity. This was just a suspicion, but I'm afraid I thought of drug money. I may have been doing the owner a gross injustice, but it had that feel to me. And that was when the idea for this story occurred to me. What if somebody came back to his island, dripping in money? What if somebody on the island took moral exception to him?

I changed the setting, and it became an island off

Scotland's west coast. Yet all islands have something in common: people take a close interest in the affairs of others, and, in some cases at least, there are people who don't like to see others getting away with things they should not get away with. In Scotland, our Calvinist background underlines that. We still believe that people should pay for their transgressions. We still disapprove. We still rather enjoy seeing tall poppies cut down where they stand. All of which might deter a gangster from considering taking up residence on the Hebridean island of Mull.

VENGEANCE

IS

MINE

Murdo had a fishing boat. At twenty-eight feet, it was not considered a large one, but it was a good sea-keeper, and he could venture out, if he so desired, in all but the most severe weather. Down below was a Ford Dover marine diesel engine, over thirty years old, that had never once declined to start; nor had it ever faltered for a moment in its constant, patient thudding. "The boat's heartbeat," he said of that sound.

He lived on Mull, an island off the west coast of Scotland. To the north lay Skye and its attendant small isles – Rum, Eigg, Canna, and the evocatively named Muck. The small isles were home to a handful of people – fifteen, in the case of Canna, while Muck somehow supported enough to have a tiny school, with a single teacher. Murdo's island was considerably bigger and had a population of several thousand people, living on farms and smallholdings dotted amongst its hills and modest glens. There was one town, Tobermory, and a smattering of villages. Here and there, harbours tucked away on the island's jagged coast were home to a small number of fishing vessels, of which Murdo's boat, the *Iolaire*, was one. *Iolaire* means "eagle" in Gaelic, and Murdo had a sea eagle, wings wide in flight, painted just off the bow, on the port side. The painting was the work of his cousin's son, who fancied himself as an artist but was not very good at portraying birds, or anything else, really. The eagle seemed to have only one eye and its talons were far from aquiline, resembling, some said, the feet of a greylag goose. But Murdo was loyal and would hear no criticism of his nephew's artistic endeavours.

Murdo's house was no more than a stone's throw from the harbour in which he kept the *Iolaire*. The village itself was on the west side of the island, looking out past a cluster of small islets – mostly tidal rocks – towards the Treshnish Isles and then to Coll. Beyond that was the Sea of the Hebrides, the stretch of water known as the Minch, and the final outposts of Scotland, the outer isles of Barra, Mingulay, the Uists, and, as a lonely afterthought, the abandoned isles of St Kilda. Then there was nothing until Canada, across mile upon mile of empty Atlantic, vast, cold fields on which pelagic fish were hunted.

Murdo was forty-eight and had the strength and robust health of one who spent his life out of doors, earning his living under an open sky. Unlike some of the islanders, whose fondness for whisky was well known, Murdo was temperate in his drinking habits. He liked peaty whiskies from the distilleries of Islay, to the south, but he would never take more than a single dram on any evening, and he always diluted whisky with water, an act of chemistry that he said improved both liquids considerably.

He had been married once but now described himself as a bachelor. It was possible that he was divorced: his wife, Helen, had served him with papers to that effect, but he had tossed them aside unread. He had no time for lawyers and their wiles. It made no difference to him. She had assured him that she would never ask him for money, as she was well provided for by her new partner, the proprietor of a successful fish-and-chip van in Glasgow, and since Murdo had no intention of ever marrying again, his matrimonial status, it seemed to him, was of no significance. It was no business of the government, nor of anybody else, he thought, whether he was married or not.

He had met her at a dance in Tobermory, when he was in his early thirties. She had been working as a barmaid in a hotel, a rambling Victorian building that clung to a clifftop overlooking the Sound of Mull. One day, people said, the hotel would fall into the sea, but they were talking nonsense, as the cliff edge was a good way away and had shown no sign of getting any closer. Helen was six years younger than he was and came from Gourock, a town on the Clyde, not far from Glasgow. She had been given the job at the hotel on the strength of her appearance – she was strikingly good-looking, in a rather blousy way, prompting the hotel manager to whisper to his wife, "Barmaid material, if ever there was. Put her behind the bar, and we're in business."

After they had married and settled back in the village, Helen quickly became bored. Her job now was to drive the day's catch to the other side of the island, where it would be loaded on a boat that plied regularly between Mull and Oban. She did not like this work, which she said should be done by a man. "I'm not designed to howk fish about," she said.

He laughed at that. There were all those old photographs of women carrying fish baskets on their backs uncomplainingly. She must have seen them. "Remember the herring girls? Remember them? They did all that work up and down the coast. No complaint from them, was there?"

She pouted. "Poor women," she said and shook her head.

"Just them?" he challenged. People were always going on about how hard it was for women, but what about men? It was hard for everybody, he thought. "What about the men? They went out in all manner of seas. Swept overboard and drowned. What about them?"

"Poor men," she said.

In spite of Helen's distaste for the work she was expected to do, they somehow got by. Then, one June, on a brilliant summer day, when Ben More, the highest mountain on the island, was sharp against the sky, she packed a suitcase and caught the bus that went over the hill. At Craignure she boarded the ferry to Oban, where she took another bus all the way down to Glasgow. There she stayed for a few days with her younger sister, having left a message for Murdo that she might be back in a few weeks' time, or might not. It was probably best, she said, for him not to expect her.

The sister was a regular at a ballroom called the Palais de Dance, one of the dance halls that injected a bit of glitter into the hard lives of working-class Glaswegians. She took Helen there three nights in a row, and on the third night she met a man called Andy McNiven.

"Andy has a fish-and-chip van," her sister said, on introducing them.

"And pies," said Andy.

"Yes, and pies," the sister confirmed.

"That's great," said Helen.

She and Andy got on well. He offered her a job in the fish-and-chip van because his wife, who had helped him for years, had gone off with a sailor from the nuclear submarine base on the Holy Loch.

After a month, Andy asked Helen to marry him. "I never actually married Maggie," he said. "People thought we were married, but we weren't. Not legally, if you see what I mean."

Helen explained that she thought that she and Murdo were probably still legally married but that she would see a lawyer and change all that. "I think you have some forms to fill in, and then you go and see the sheriff, and that's that," she said.

"Sounds simple enough," said Andy.

Some years later, a friend said to Murdo, "Looking back at it, Murdo, do you regret marrying Helen? Of course, don't answer if you think the question is too personal."

Murdo considered this for a few moments. He did not have to think for long before replying, "Not really. We weren't a brilliant match, but that wasn't her fault. I shouldn't have asked her to marry me. That's down to me. You get what you ask for, you see."

The friend frowned. "You mean – what goes around, comes around? That sort of thing."

"Aye," said Murdo. "You get what you deserve, I think. In general, that is."

The friend looked out of the window. They were in Murdo's kitchen at the time, a pot of strong tea on the table before them. "Do you think so?" he asked.

Murdo nodded. "I think so. Yes. I've always felt that. If you do something wrong, then sooner or later . . ." He shrugged. "Sooner or later, you'll suffer the consequences."

"I'm not so sure," said the friend. "I think that a lot of folk get away with it, especially these days, when everything's gone to the dogs. You know how it is – nobody cares any longer about who does what."

Murdo looked at his friend. He was right, he thought. He shook his head. "You may have a point, Donald," he said. "In the old days—"

Donald interrupted him. He smiled. "When exactly were the old days, Murdo?"

"The day before yesterday," came the answer. "When you and I were young, Donald. In the old days, if you did something you shouldn't do, you knew that you'd pay for it."

"Which is why people were a bit better behaved," mused Donald.

"Perhaps. There were policemen then . . . You saw them in the street. Even in Tobermory. There was that Constable Frazer – remember him, Donald? Big fellow with red hair. You wouldn't cross him, sure enough."

"He gave that Billy Jamieson a clip round the ear," Donald remembered. "Taught him not to help himself to other people's lobster pots."

"That was before human rights," said Murdo. "Human rights stopped that sort of . . . What do they call it? Some fancy name. Community policing?" He sighed. "Changed days. People can do pretty much as they please."

"Looks like it," said Donald. "No avenging angel. No justice. Nothing."

Donald brought the conversation back to Helen and her departure. "You've been by yourself for a long time now," he said. "Ever thought of getting yourself fixed up again?"

Murdo shook his head. "Not really. I'm all right with my own company. I'm comfortable enough." He paused. "And now I'm an elder of the kirk, you know. That keeps me busy."

Donald understood. He had heard about his friend's appointment as a church elder – it had been in the *Oban Times* – but had forgotten to congratulate him.

"That's a very important position," he said.

Murdo nodded. "The new minister is a breath of fresh air," he said. "That last fellow was too . . . How shall I put it? Too wishy-washy. I'm not sure he believed in very much. This new one has very clear ideas. He can't be doing with all this liberal theology stuff."

"This new one believes in judgement?"

"Definitely," said Murdo. "Of other people, of course."

"Of course."

"There's nothing wrong with a day of judgement," Murdo remarked. "People get uneasy these days if you start talking about that sort of thing. But just not mentioning something doesn't mean it isn't there, does it?"

It took Donald a little while to sort that question out. Then he replied, "We'll pay for it, you know. We're creating a hell for ourselves right here – let alone anything down below. People rampage around. They show no respect for anybody else. It's not right, Murdo – it's not right. We need to try to get our sense of justice back. We need to teach people that if you behave badly, you'll get it. It's as simple as that."

"You're right there," agreed Murdo.

Donald looked regretful. "Too late," he said. "Too late for any of that, Murdo. Things have . . . How do they put it these days? Things have *moved on*."

"I haven't moved on," Murdo said meditatively. "And I don't think it's too late, you know."

Donald would remember those words later on. *I don't think it's too late.*

Nor did the new minister at the church near the harbour think it was too late. He was called the Reverend Lachlan Maclean, and he came from Stornoway, on one of the largest of the outer islands. He had been brought up in a Gaelic-speaking household but was perfectly bilingual and felt as confident – and as convinced – in English as he felt in Gaelic. He was a graduate of New College, the divinity school of the University of Edinburgh and, thanks to a St Andrew's Society scholarship, of the Union Theological Seminary at Princeton. At Princeton, he had written a thesis on Calvin and won a prestigious prize for an essay on the concept of sin, subsequently published under the title *The Rehabilitation of Sin*. The Reverend Maclean was in no doubt about the existence of sin, and he strongly disputed the notion that wrongdoing was a relative notion, its contours defined by individual preference. "We all know exactly what sin is," he said, with that directness for which he was widely admired. "Sins, you see, are things you shouldn't do, and we all know what those things are. They are the same for all times and all places, and for all men. No problem there, if you ask me. That's about as clear as anything ever can be."

The Reverend Maclean had no time for modernisers. He was particularly appalled by efforts to prune the hymnary of wordings and concepts that might be considered old-fashioned. In the view of some of these modernisers, all references to the Devil should be removed from hymns or liturgy, as there was no real reason to conclude that such a being as the Devil actually existed. "The fools," pronounced the Reverend Maclean. "Saying that the Devil doesn't exist is exactly what he wants you to say. Make no mistake about that. Beelzebub kens these things fine. That's the precise script he'd write for us if he had the time. These people don't realise it, but they are playing right into his sulphurous hands." He paused. "And when they die – those so-called liberal theologians – oh, my goodness, are they going to suffer. It almost makes feel sympathetic towards them, but then I remind myself – they had it coming to them."

Murdo enjoyed the Reverend Maclean's sermons. He did not mind their length – they lasted, on average, just under an hour – as they were firm in their disapproval of everything that he happened to disapprove of himself: moral relativism, first and foremost, and then, in no particular order, immodest clothing, vulgar television, badly behaved children, London, Roman Catholicism, Sunday football, and a variety of other issues on which the fringes of Scotland were at odds with the zeitgeist. As he sat there and listened to the minister's condemnation of these insidious influences, Murdo found himself imagining what it would be like locally were the dreadful day of judgement to dawn, as clearly promised in the scriptures. He had no doubt but that he and the Reverend Maclean would be spared the divine retribution – not to say revenge – that would be visited on the land, but he had his doubts about some others, including a few of his neighbours. There would certainly be some gnashing of teeth in the bars of Tobermory as the drinkers and wastrels were driven out into the street to face the brimstone awaiting them; and there was that deckhand on the MacBrayne's ferry who was always flirting outrageously with the female passengers – he would have something to answer for on that day. Oh, he would grovel and apologise, but it would be too late, and he would be tipped down into the infernal regions of perpetual fire. It would all be very satisfactory, and it gave Murdo a warm feeling to picture it, even though he knew that it was, unfortunately, rather unlikely to occur in his own lifetime. People had been waiting for the dreadful day of judgement for years now, and it had never arrived. It was most disheartening.

Murdo knew that the local sinners were hardly a patch on some of the sinners you encountered in places like Glasgow and, even more so, London. Paris, too, was another place where sinners were thick on the ground. He had heard that France in general was a dreadful place for sinning, and quite shameless about it. Of course, they were French, and the French had had nobody like John Knox to set them straight. They were hedonists, through and through, sitting about in their cafés, drinking coffee, and talking about the sort of thing that the French like to talk about. They would pay for it eventually, he was sure, but in the meantime he had to admit that they seemed to be having rather a good time.

Murdo felt that although there were undoubtedly some sinners on Mull, there were not all that many, and none of them were really conspicuously evil. One spring day, though, everything changed, and a significant sinner – the real McCoy – arrived on Mull and announced his intention of staying. This was news, and it travelled quickly up and down the island, eventually reaching Murdo as he tied the *Iolaire* to the harbour pier and began to unload his iced and already crated catch.

A farmhouse just outside the village had been on the market for some time. Now, Murdo heard, it had been bought, and the new owner had already been to inspect it before the painters moved in. Donald gave Murdo this news as he watched him hosing down his deck with the harbour hose.

"The new owner is not short of cash," said Donald. "He's from Fort William originally. Name of McCoy. I've heard about him from folk up there. Not good."

Murdo frowned. "Why's he coming here, then? What's wrong with Fort William?"

"I'm told they don't want him there," said Donald. "I'm told that the boys over there didn't want him about the place."

"If the boys don't want you . . ."

"Yes. And these were boys he had been at school with, mind."

Murdo looked thoughtful. "Sometimes people are envious of success. If this boy went off somewhere and made his fortune, they might not like it back home. You know what people are like."

Donald did, but he quickly pointed out that this situation was not at all like that. "He went down south," he explained. "London. Then he was in Miami, I believe. He came back a rich man."

Murdo waited. It was not unheard of for people to

go to America and return with a newly minted fortune in their pockets. There was money to be made over there, as Andrew Carnegie was to discover. Now Donald said, "Dirty money. None of it was legally acquired."

Murdo raised an eyebrow. "From?"

"Night clubs. Shady deals. That sort of thing."

"So, he was a gangster?" Murdo asked.

"So I've heard," said Donald.

Murdo grimaced. "Not the sort we want around here."

"No," said Donald. "Definitely not."

Then Murdo asked, "Have you met him yet?"

Donald shook his head. "I saw him when he was going up to take a look at the place. You could hardly miss his car – a muckle red Bentley. Sleekit. Long as your boat."

"Red?"

"Yes. Fire-engine red. It must have cost" – he shrugged before continuing – "hundreds of thousands."

"Not an honest car, then?"

Donald smiled. "Definitely not."

Murdo finished hosing down his deck. He looked up and saw that in the distance, just coming into view, there was a large, red car. "Speak of the Devil," he said.

Robert R. McCoy, widely known as Rob Roy McCoy, drove his red Bentley Continental along the unpaved road that led to the farmhouse previously known as Tattie Mains but now dignified with the name South Ness House. He noted the bad condition of this road – which he now owned. Potholes, some of them filled with water that disguised their full extent, occurred every few yards, and here and there the rains had completely destroyed the camber. He had already spoken to a contractor, who had agreed to bring over a grader to sort out the problem, but until then the road was a serious threat to his Bentley's suspension.

The car was his pride and joy – a trophy, really, the most tangible sign of his success in life. He had bought it new in Edinburgh and driven it over to Fort William when he went back there to look up some of his old friends. That had not been a successful visit. He had intended to buy a house in the area and then to open a hotel or bar – not that he needed to, but in order to give him something to do. The coolness of his welcome, though, had persuaded him otherwise, and in impulse he had chosen to buy the house and its accompanying three hundred acres on the west coast of Mull.

Now he was here to spend a few months doing the place up and preparing it for when his long-term girlfriend, Kitty, arrived from Florida. She was a native of Belfast but had no desire to live in Ireland. "Scotland I can just about manage, Robbie," she said. "But Ireland, no. Never going back there. Never, but." It was an Ulster habit to add the word "but" to a comment, and Kitty did that frequently.

He had told her about Mull, and she had been lukewarm but came round to his view of things when he explained that they could divide their time between Mull and Marbella. Kitty did not like the heat, and so they would spend the summers in Mull, where it was always cool, and the winters in Marbella, when the temperature would be comfortable and not too extreme.

On this particular trip, Rob was to meet the interior decorator he had chosen to decorate their new home. Kitty was not particularly interested in such matters and had asked only that the living room should feature a bar with stools upholstered in zebra skin, or an artificial fabric representing zebra skin. "I'm not sure if zebras still exist," she had said to Rob. "Are they extinct yet, Robbie?"

Rob was not sure. "Perhaps," he said. "But you can still get zebra skin, I think."

"And the pool," she said, "I'd like that in a sort of conservatory. Make it infinity, like that pool we had in Florida, in the first house. I loved swimming right up to the edge and looking out towards the . . ." She faltered at that. Kitty was geographically challenged and was not quite sure of the name of the sea over which she had looked from her infinity pool.

"Caribbean," supplied Rob. "It's your actual Caribbean over there, Kitty."

"Whatever," said Kitty. "You'll know what I mean, but."

The decorator, who was due to arrive the following day, was called Bambi Trefoil. She lived in London and had decorated the Essex home of one of Rob's contacts, Tommy Jones. Tommy was unfortunately in prison now and unable to enjoy the luxurious surroundings that

Bambi had prepared for him, but he took comfort in the knowledge that these were awaiting him on his release.

Rob was not going to interfere too much. Bambi had assured him that she would obtain all the furniture and fabrics needed to transform South Ness House into a suitable home for a man of his status. She would source these, she said – she used the word "source" as a verb a great deal – from a variety of suppliers and was confident that he would approve of what she provided.

Rob was intending to use local contractors as far as was possible, as he felt that it was important to show willing to support the local economy. Although he was from Fort William, which was on the mainland and not on Mull, he still thought of himself as a local boy in these parts and he would not want people to think he had forgotten that. This plan, though, proved to be difficult to execute, as local contractors, for whatever reason, seemed unwilling to tender for the work.

"Not touching that with a bargepole," said one. "Thanks very much."

"I've put the work out to a whole range of local builders," his architect said. "But not one of them seems interested. Odd, that. You'd think they'd jump at the work."

Rob shrugged. He was indifferent to petty local opposition. Who were these people? Nobody. His car cost as much as their houses – possibly more. They should think about that from time to time. "Bring people in from Glasgow," he'd said. "Put them up at the local hotel. There are plenty of contractors down in Glasgow who'll take this on."

That proved to be the case, and for the last six weeks a variety of contractors – plumbers, plasterers, roofers, and joiners – had been working away to make the house ready for Bambi's finishing touches.

"My blank canvas," said Bambi, as Rob showed her round after her arrival. "The ideas are *flooding* into my head, Rob – flooding."

He had booked her into a hotel a few miles outside the village. He was staying in the house, in the main bedroom, in which there was already a bed and wardrobe, both obtained by Bambi.

"I sourced the wardrobe in the Chilterns," she said. "There's a dear little place there that sells French furniture. I just love it – love it to pieces. And the bed is pure Napoleon – pure Napoleon. *Très* imperial, Rob, as you'll have noticed."

They ate lunch together in the kitchen, on a table that Bambi had sourced in Inverness, with cutlery sourced from an auction in Perth. They had a steak and kidney pie sourced from the supermarket in Tobermory.

"So romantic," enthused Bambi. "*Déjeuner sur l'herbe*, almost. If we were outside, if you see what I mean."

"Cool," said Rob.

"Your name," Bambi said, looking at him over the rim of her wine glass, "wasn't there an earlier Rob Roy? Where have I heard of him?"

"There was," said Rob. "There was Rob Roy MacGregor. He was something of a wild man, but Scotland was pretty wild in those days. Everyone was an outlaw, more or less.'

"So romantic," Bambi repeated. "That's what I like about this country. The romance. The mountains. Waterfalls. Sheep. It's all to die for."

On the third day of Bambi Trefoil's visit, Rob decided that he had fallen in love with her.

"As you know," he said, "I'm in a relationship. But I've been reviewing that, and I think it's time for me to come out of that relationship. I need to ask myself where I'm going in life."

This was what Bambi had been hoping to hear. She secretly liked rough, decisive men. And rough, decisive men who were also conspicuously solvent struck her as being particularly attractive. "You mean you need to *emerge*?" she said.

That was exactly right, thought Rob. "Yes, I need to emerge. And I think I am, you know. I think I am emerging."

Bambi listened. "I feel very much the same. I'm sort of mixed up with Trefoil, as you know, but he and I have got to the end of our mutual journey, I think. We've explored; we've flourished. But now we need to let one another go. We have to. It's a question of space for growth. And I'd be the last person – the very last – to deny him that space. I really mean that, you know."

"Space for growth is very important," agreed Rob.

He was a fast learner, and he had acquired a facility with the sort of terminology Bambi liked to use. "You have to be free to fulfil your inner potential."

"You're so perceptive," said Bambi. "We speak the same language, I feel."

"Fate," said Rob. "You know what I get when I look at you and me, Bambi? I get *future*."

The following day, Rob sent a text message to Kitty. *Don't come after all*, he said. *I need a bit of space. Let's cool things for a while.* This was followed by an emoticon – a smiling face – and an "x".

She phoned him that afternoon. "Okay, Rob, tell me straight: it's Bambi, isn't it?"

He hesitated, but only for a few moments. "Yes," he said.

"So, it's about sex? Right?"

He drew in his breath. "No need to be crude," he said.

There was silence. Rob heard her breathing. Then she said, "If that's the way you want it, then that's the way you want it."

He said, "I'm glad that we can be grown up about it."

Relieved that this was dealt with, he took Bambi out for a drive in the red Bentley Continental.

"Lovely motor," said Bambi appreciatively.

They drove over to Tobermory, where Bambi sourced a scarf and a box of Scottish confectionary known as tablet. They each ate a piece as they sat in the Bentley, the radio tuned to a hard rock station in Glasgow. People walking past stared at them with disapproval. They knew who Rob was. This was an island, and people knew.

One of the passers-by was the Reverend Lachlan Maclean, who was in Tobermory to do his weekly shop at the supermarket. He slowed down as he walked past the Bentley. He frowned. Rob caught his eye. He knew who the Reverend Maclean was. He smiled, but the minister turned his head away quickly and continued on his way to the supermarket.

"Who's that?" asked Bambi.

"The local minister," said Rob. "They're always like that. Miserable bunch. Sense of fun? Forget it!"

"He gave you a bit of a look," said Bambi. "Did you see it? Maybe he didn't like our music."

"Envy," replied Rob. "I'm used to it." Then he expanded, "You go off and make a bit of money. Then you come back, and what do you get? Envy! That's Scotland for you, Bambi."

Bambi nodded. Then she said, as if thinking of something for the first time, "I don't think I ever asked you, Rob: where did you make your money?"

Rob licked fragments of tablet off his fingers. "My money?"

"Yes." She gestured at the car around her; at the white leather upholstery; at the walnut fascia.

He tapped the side of his nose. "Business."

She looked at him. "But what sort of business?"

"Arranging things," said Rob. "Import, export. Think: deals."

"You were a sort of middleman? You sourced things?"

Rob nodded. That, he thought, would do. "I sometimes sourced things. Yes, I sourced."

"It's very satisfying, isn't it?"

Rob laughed. "Sourcing? Yes, it is. And lucrative."

"Getting people what they want is a real calling," observed Bambi. "That's how I view my own work, you know. I see a need in people – a need for beauty in their surroundings. And I give them what they are . . . what they are *yearning* for." She paused. "It's all about yearning, isn't it, Rob?"

He agreed.

Two months passed. Now it was early August, and an area of high pressure settled over that part of Scotland, bringing long, warm days and a flat sea. Murdo went out fishing three days a week, but on other days he would make himself available for charter to small groups of visitors who wished to visit Fingal's Cave on Staffa, or cruise out to the Treshnish Isles in the hope of spotting basking sharks. There were birdwatchers, too, who were keen to see puffins and the other sea-birds that bred around that part of the coast. Murdo's boat was not ideal for these purposes, as it was slow and smelled permanently of fish, but these drawbacks added to the authenticity of the experience for those visitors who liked to drop a line for mackerel and quiz Murdo on the life of a real fisherman.

These outings were arranged through the nearby hotel, where a small notice informed guests that:

Small party sea trips can be arranged with a local skipper.

See the miracle of Fingal's Cave that inspired Mendelssohn!

Watch basking sharks as they filter plankton through their great jaws!

See the colourful puffins bob up and down on waves!

And it was on one of these trips that Kitty went after she had arrived at the hotel, having booked herself in for a week.

She was discreet, keeping to herself and taking her meals in the privacy of her room. During the day, she took walks along the shore, picking up and discarding shells and odd bits of driftwood. Her only outing was the booking she made for Murdo's boat, on which she planned to go out to Staffa.

Murdo was used to having at least three or four guests on the boat and found it strange to have just one. At first, there was little conversation, but after an hour or two, when they were well out to sea and the sun had come out from behind a cloud, Kitty began to talk.

"There's somebody living near here," she said. "A man by the name of McCoy. They call him Rob Roy sometimes."

Murdo inclined his head. He was not one to give too much away. "Could be," he said.

"Do you know him?" she asked.

He answered her with a question of his own. "Do you?"

She looked out across the gentle swell of the sea. "I do, as it happens."

He was watching her. "He's from Fort William originally. He hasn't been long in these parts."

She nodded. "I'm not surprised. He's on the run, you know. He's a gangster."

Murdo's eyes widened. This confirmed everything he had thought about Rob. "That car of his . . ." he began.

Her expression was one of disgust. "How do you think he bought that?"

Murdo let out a whistle of surprise. "I see. Well, a car like that couldn't be bought with honest money."

"No."

Murdo looked at her. "How do you know this?" he asked.

"I'm a police officer," lied Kitty.

Murdo's eyes grew wider.

"Our problem, though," Kitty went on, "is that we have no proof. We can't make a case against him. You know how these people are – they cover their tracks." She sighed. "So, I'm going to have to go back down to London empty-handed. That's it."

She watched his reaction. Then she said, in a tone of regret, "I sometimes think it's a great pity that local people can't take things into their own hands. You know – deal with people like that in their own way. You'd think they might be able to come up with some way of showing such people the door."

Murdo said nothing. They could see Staffa now. Off their starboard bow, a large white sea-bird, yellow-beaked, circled higher and higher, until it dropped into the water like a stone.

"Gannet," muttered Murdo. "They enter the water at sixty miles an hour, you know. Sixty."

He was thinking.

The Reverend Lachlan Maclean sat in his sparsely furnished study. It was not a comfortable room – there was a desk, a metal filing cabinet, and a large, glass-fronted bookcase. There were three straight-backed chairs – one for the minister, and two for visitors. There were no rugs on the floor. On the wall behind the desk there was a picture of the Mount of Olives.

Murdo had put on a suit to visit the minister. The jacket was ill-fitting, as it had belonged to his father, who was a man of stouter build. The trousers, which had large turn-ups on the legs, were shiny at the knees.

The Reverend Maclean had fixed his cold blue eyes on Murdo. Neither was speaking. Then the minister broke the silence. "How very kind of her," he said.

Murdo nodded. "She has no particular connection with Mull," he said. "But she so appreciated the peacefulness of her stay here."

"And you say she's now gone?"

"Yes, she had to return to London."

"What a pity," said the Reverend Maclean. "I would have liked to have thanked her personally." He paused. "It's a very generous gift. Two thousand pounds is no small amount."

Murdo agreed. "I'm sure that the parish treasurer will find it useful," he said.

"Very," agreed the Reverend Maclean. He looked bemused. "And all this happened as a direct result of a trip out to Staffa?"

"Yes," said Murdo. "Sometimes I find that people are changed by the beauty of the sea. And the quiet, I suppose. It makes them think about their priorities."

"That's something we all need to do," agreed the Reverend Maclean. "We should examine ourselves regularly. We should open ourselves to grace."

"Yes," said Murdo. "We should do that, I think."

They looked at one another.

Mrs Sumner, the widow of the former harbourmaster, and a stalwart of the church, whispered to her friend, Mrs Brodie, as they waited for the service to begin the following Sunday.

"Have you heard, Bessie? Have you heard the news?"

Mrs Brodie had not.

"Well, I'll tell you," said Mrs Sumner. "You know that man with the car – that great big red car? That one?"

"Aye, I ken him. Not a nice piece of work, I hear. A gangster, they say."

"So I've heard. And his past is catching up with him. My daughter cleans the house for him, you know."

Mrs Brodie waited.

"And you wouldn't believe it, but he found a sheep's head on his pillow. Blood all over the place."

"No!"

"He did. He was terrified, apparently. Packed up immediately. But then his car went on fire. Shot up in flames. Nothing left, apparently – just the chassis."

"No!"

"Yes!"

"And he's gone now?"

"Yes, he hired a car from Tobermory and that's him away. And that woman of his, too."

Mrs Brodie shook her head. "Well, well . . ."

She was unable to finish what she was saying as the Reverend Maclean was now rising to his feet. He cleared his throat.

"Good people," he said. "My text today is Romans 12:19, where it is written, *Do not avenge yourselves, but rather give place to wrath, for it is written 'Vengeance is mine: I shall repay'.*"

It was a good sermon – one of the Reverend Maclean's best, thought Murdo. After the service, he and two other elders joined the Reverend Maclean and his wife for a Sunday lunch: lamb chops. Sourced by the minister himself.

A MELBOURNE STORY

An Introduction

Melbourne is a favourite city of mine. This story is set in Fitzroy North, a suburb of the city, a place of small bungalows with tin roofs, shady verandas, and, in some cases, ornate French ironwork. In such a place I have imagined a drama school, not entirely dissimilar to the dance academy in which I was obliged, as an unwilling teenager, to learn ballroom dancing. There was French chalk there on the wooden floor, and there were sluggish ceiling fans that barely disturbed the air. My teacher used to drag on a cigarette as she taught me the quick step and the cha-cha. She blew the smoke over my shoulder. That was how things were in those days.

The revenge here is sought in the world of actors. Now, actors are no worse nor better morally than the ordinary run of humanity, but they do tend a bit more towards backbiting and petty jealousy than people who follow other callings. Or not (a necessary qualification, to avert howls of protest from my actor friends). Perhaps it would be fairer to say that we are all liable to feel jealousy of those who succeed when we may fail to do so. We may pretend to welcome the success of others, but do we really accept it? Do we prefer failure?

As Gore Vidal thought, we might die a little every time a friend succeeds.

Actors, in general, make good friends. They kiss you warmly and without provocation. They use the term "darling" to all, without any attention as to the length of time they have known the other person. Even dogs are called darling. They sign off their letters with the words "Oceans of love". By and large, they mean it.

THE PRINCIPLES

of

SOAP

*"Brecht is all very well, but most of us, if we are honest,
will admit that we still take pleasure in a well-crafted
soap."*

– George Peters,
Thirty Years of Film and Television
(I can find no record of this publication, which is not
surprising, as it is entirely made up)

David Thoreau was an actor – not a particularly good
one, but not as bad as some. "Look," he said, "I
know where I am on the talent spectrum. Some people
are up there" – he raised a hand above his head, the
realm of the Oliviers, the Streeps – "while some people
are down there." And he pointed to the ground, the
realm of the pantomime artists, the single-line extras,
the members of the chorus line. "I'm somewhere in the

middle." And with that he smiled. There is a particular pleasure in knowing exactly where one fits in – and accepting it.

He came from a former gold-mining town in Victoria. The gold had run out a long time ago, but the seams that rippled beneath the undulating Australian countryside had lasted long enough and been sufficiently productive to leave the town with an attractive civic centre, an impressive library, and two well-designed golf courses. Farming became once again the mainstay of the local economy, and the town's annual agricultural show attracted visitors from throughout the state. It was a good place in which to grow up, to raise a family, and then to grow old, playing golf and attending the popular bingo sessions in the country club. It was, however, very dull, and anybody of any imagination or ambition tended to leave the town at the age of eighteen, when they went off to one of the large cities, for work or education. Very few people stayed behind unless they went into a family business or took on a family farm.

David had always wanted to act. It started, his mother later said, when he was chosen to play the role of Joseph in the local kindergarten's nativity play – a role that he threw himself into with considerable vigour. Joseph was never intended to steal Mary's limelight, but that is how David tackled the role, elbowing Mary out of the way in the stable scene and brushing off the Three Wise Men before snatching their gifts. At the end, when applause broke out and the children took a bow, Joseph moved swiftly to the foreground, pushing Mary into the crib and breaking the spindly leg of one of the papier mâché sheep.

"That boy's going far," muttered a bemused member of the audience.

"Real ambition there," agreed another, adding, "And there's talent too."

And there was – at least at the level of the school drama club. Year after year saw David playing the lead part in the school plays, and so, when the time came for him to choose a career, there was really very little question about what he would do.

"I'm going on the stage," he told his parents. "Professionally, that is. I want to be a famous actor."

His father glanced at his mother before he addressed his son. They both wanted him to be an accountant, which was what his father was, although not a particularly successful one. "The theatre's difficult, son," he said evenly, trying to sound as if he were dispensing dispassionate advice. "A lot of people want to act, but hardly any of them make it. Such a shame, but there we are. Those are the facts. Always look at the facts."

David reeled off five or six household names.

"Oh, yes, they made it all right," said his father. "But how many hundreds of their contemporaries didn't? Thousands, I'd say."

"You know something, David?" chipped in his mother. "They work as waiters."

She looked at him as if she had just imparted a dreadful warning. Now she continued, "Most waiters went to drama college, you know. Nobody goes to waiting college. It's drama you study if you want to be a waiter."

David closed his eyes. What did his parents know? Nothing. Zilch. Nada.

"How many waiters do you know who are really accountants?" she continued. And then, turning to her husband, she said, "Do you know any accountants, Dick – any – who have to work as waiters?"

"Not off the top of my head, Lil," he replied.

David stared at his parents. They were not bad, as parents went – he could easily have done worse, he thought – but they really had no idea of what was what in the theatre. Of course, he knew that it was a competitive world, but the people who ended up as waiters were the ones with no talent, who should never have tried to go on the stage in the first place. He was different. He did not wish to be boastful, but who had been chosen for the lead role in every single school play for the last six years? He had. And who, after sending an enquiry letter, had received an encouraging response from the Roger Dare Acting Studio in Melbourne informing him that places were available on the one-year full-time acting course starting in February? This course, it was explained, introduced the student to all the skills that were necessary to audition successfully for theatrical and film roles both in Australia and abroad. Many of the school's graduates had gone on to stellar careers in London or Los Angeles. "The sky," the school's brochure claimed, "is the limit when you train with Roger Dare. *Dare to be great!* is our motto. Make it yours: contact us about enrolment today. Please remember to send a (recent) photograph."

David had shown the brochure to his father. "See here, Dad," he said. "See those quotes there – they're from past students who have all got acting jobs. See what they say. Just read it, Dad. That's all I ask."

His father glanced at the glossy brochure. "Why do they ask you to send a photograph?" he asked suspiciously. "You see what it says there? It says, *Please send a photograph.* Why do they need a photograph to decide if you can act?"

David humoured his father. He was so *yesterday*. He had *no idea*.

"They need it because if you want to be an actor you have to be . . . well, you have to look the part, see. They don't want people who maybe have only one ear, say."

"Why would they have only one ear? Who's only got one ear?"

David was patient. You had to be patient with your parents. "I'm not saying anybody in particular only has one ear," he replied. "I'm not saying that. That was just an example. And maybe there are people who have a really gross nose. There may not be all that many parts for people with really gross noses. It might be better for them to do something else. That's all that the photograph means."

The application duly went off, strongly supported by the drama teacher from the local school. *This young man*, she wrote, *has been the mainstay of our drama programme for the past six years. His performance as King Lear last year is still being talked about, and the leading part he played in our* Tribute to Mime *program was even mentioned in the local newspaper. With the right advice and assistance, I am confident that he will, in due course, mature into an actor of some consequence.*

Seeing this glowing reference, David's father wondered whether he had perhaps been too ready to write off acting as a career for his son. "We may have to eat our words," he confided to Lil. "I'm rarely wrong, but there it is in black and white: *an actor of some consequence.* That means only one thing to me: our David can act."

"Seems like it," said Lil. She looked thoughtful. "Where he gets it from is anybody's guess. None of my family were actors. They were mostly sheep people."

"Strange," mused her husband. "But then I suppose it's often like that with people of talent." He smiled. "Did Mr and Mrs da Vinci say to one another, 'Where does our boy get his ability to draw?'"

"Who knows, Dick?" she replied. "They say that when you have children you never know what you're going to get."

"True," he said. "You don't."

"And we've ended up with an actor."

"So it seems, Lil. So it seems."

That was in 1996, when David was a month or so short of his eighteenth birthday. That was a bit young, his parents felt, to live entirely independently in Melbourne, and so his mother arranged for him to stay with her cousin, Nell, in Fitzroy North. Nell, a piano teacher and widow of a radio engineer, had a red brick Federation-style bungalow with wide pillars at each end of the veranda. The house had a postage stamp-sized garden in the front, intersected by an uneven paved path. Along the edges of the path there were small cement casts of cockleshells painted white and pink. The gate through which access was gained to this path was of wrought iron, with a fleur-de-lys motif. That, Nell explained, was because the first occupants had been a French couple who owned a lace importing business. In her view, that fact, along with the fleur-de-lys adornments, gave the house a certain continental sophistication, reflected, should other associations be missed, in its name: Montmartre.

There was more than enough room for a lodger, as some years ago the house had been extended at the back, where the kitchen gave out onto an ill-kept patch of lawn, and from there onto a narrow sanitary lane. A garage had been added to the end of the back garden, and this was occupied by a car belonging to a neighbour – Nell did not drive – and by various garden implements. There was something uncomfortable about this garage – something in its atmosphere – that David picked up immediately when Nell first showed him round.

"I don't like to go in here at night," she said. "There used to be a light, but it doesn't work any longer. I think there is some sort of presence – not that I believe in such things. But I still get an odd feeling when I'm here."

David agreed. "Maybe something happened here," he said. "A long time ago. Something bad that has left its trace. There are places where that happens. Hanging Rock and places like that."

"You don't need to come out here," said Nell. "Jimmy Gordon next door takes his car out from time to time; otherwise nobody sets foot in it. Best ignored, if you ask me."

The house itself had a very different atmosphere. Nell was untidy, and a bit of a hoarder. As it happened, she liked the theatre, and there were shelves of books on theatrical subjects and box after box of old programmes from the Athenaeum Theatre on Collins Street. Nell was a regular frequenter of the Athenaeum shows, especially musicals, of which she knew the words to all the songs. "There is nothing to beat *My Fair Lady*," she said to David as she poured him tea on that first afternoon. "Perhaps you'll be able to study it at the Roger Dare – who knows?" She looked at him fondly. "I don't want to raise anybody's hopes too much, but I wonder when we'll see you, David, on the stage of the Athenaeum? No, don't blush. There's every chance. You must have the talent, or you wouldn't have been accepted by Dare's. They don't take everyone, you know. I've heard of plenty of young people who have tried to get in there, but no luck. Plenty."

"I don't know," said David. "We'll see."

He was confident, though, that the Athenaeum would only be a first step. He was thinking more of the West End of London or Broadway, even of Hollywood. It might take a bit of time, but he was convinced that he had it in him. You could either act or you could not – and he could.

She showed him to his room, which was at the front of the house. It had net curtains, a writing table, and a straight-backed chair. The bed was high and narrow and had the look of a hospital bed. The bedspread was a thick cotton sheet on which had been printed the words of Kipling's poem "If".

"To inspire you," said Nell, and laughed.

The following day he made his way by tram to the converted fire station that housed the Roger Dare Studio. An introductory session was to be held at ten, after the new intake of students had registered and been given their timetable and coursework materials for the first term. Then, in the main practice hall, they met Roger Dare himself, a dapper figure in his late forties, wearing a striped blazer of the sort favoured by rowing crews. A red silk cravat around his neck, he held in his right hand an ebony cigarette holder in which no cigarette was placed. There were nicotine stains in the small sandy-coloured moustache he had cultivated above his upper lip.

"Today," he said to the assembled group of thirty students, "is a new beginning for each and every one of you. It is the first day of your theatrical careers – a day that some years from now, I imagine, you will remember and ask yourself: did I understand then, on that morning all those years ago when I first signed up at drama school, what a great adventure I was embarking upon? And the answer you will give, I suspect, is that you did not, because nobody knows at your stage of life just what they are letting themselves in for when they set out to become an actor. This is not just any career. This is not the same as being an accountant, or a nurse, or a fireman – as you will have seen, this is an old fire station. This is a *calling* – the equivalent of joining a monastery or going off to an ashram in India. This is *enlisting* in a body of men and women who dedicate their lives to the stage. You give your life to that, you know – you don't give just part of it, you give your whole life. You become an actor in your *soul* as well as in your sinews. Being an actor is what you *are*, not just how you happen to earn your living. And that bit – the earning of a living – is never going to be anything but tough. The theatre may bring great rewards to some – my friend David Niven was one of those who did rather well . . ."

David drew in his breath. He was in the same room as somebody who knew David Niven. The closest he had come to such greatness was the librarian at school whose uncle had met Noël Coward.

". . . and the same might be said of my good friend Peter Finch, who did well enough too. But for most actors, there is no fortune waiting to be made. There may be a living, but it is unlikely to be a very generous one. But does that matter? I don't think it does. What matters is being backstage, waiting to go on, hearing the hum of the audience out there, and then that moment, that glorious moment, when you go out on stage and every eye in the house is on *you*. And that is when I hope you say to yourself, 'Going to the Roger Dare was the best thing I ever did in my life.' Is that too much for me to hope? I don't think so. And why do I say that? I say it because there have been more students than I can remember who have said that exact thing to me. And each time I have heard it, I have felt the same flush of pride as I feel right now, talking to you here this morning, as you are about to begin your course. That is what I feel, ladies and gentlemen – that is what I feel in my heart."

Roger Dare stopped. He looked down at his cigarette holder, which David saw was shaking. He took it from his right hand with his left, and then put it between his lips, still without a cigarette. He looked up at the ceiling, and the lights were upon his nicotine-stained moustache and the shoulders of his striped blazer. One of the students began to clap, tentatively, but was soon joined by the others. There were murmurs of appreciation as well. Roger Dare brought his gaze down from the ceiling and let it move across the faces of his students, as if assessing each one.

David glanced at the young man sitting next to him, who looked back at him and smiled. "Mr Dare's a great actor," he said.

"No," said David. "I don't think he was acting."

They introduced themselves. The student next to David was called Henry. His father was a grazier. Henry had gone to Geelong Grammar and applied to study drama at the University of Sydney before he had heard of the Roger Dare. "Those university courses are not about acting," he said. "They're about drama. Shakespeare and so on. I want to *act*."

"What in?" asked David.

"Television series," said Henry. "I see myself in a police show. Long-running. And you?"

"Theatre," said David.

"*Hamlet*?"

"Yes, but other roles too. I like *Macbeth*."

"Tragic," said Henry. "She was the one who pushed him into it, you know. I don't think he would have done it if it hadn't been for her."

Roger Dare was now announcing the day's programme. "We're going to start with a limbering-up," he said. "That's how we'll start every day. Physicality, ladies and gentlemen – that's the first thing you need to get on top of. Inhabit your body. Your body is *you*. Make it a partner in a *unity* of expression and *being*."

They had been instructed to bring loose-fitting exercise clothing. Now they changed into these and then re-assembled in the hall to begin their limbering-up session. Music was played, and they were encouraged to dance. David noticed that Henry was somewhat clumsy. Roger Dare noticed that too. "You're Henry, right?" he said. "Well, Henry, I want you to try to overcome a certain stiffness in your gait. Loosen up. Really loose. Nobody's looking at you, you know."

But David saw that Henry was being watched by one of the young women. They were all wearing name badges, and he could see that she was called Virginia. She had a cruel mouth, he thought, and seemed to be smiling at Henry's awkwardness. When she saw that David was looking at her, Virginia looked away sharply. David thought, She's my enemy. He was surprised to find himself thinking that, because he was naturally affable and did not easily make enemies. But he did not like her. He glanced at Henry, who smiled back at him and continued with his stiff, un-coordinated movements. Perhaps he would loosen up in due course, thought David. And there was more to acting than simply being fluid in one's movements; Henry must have other talents to have been admitted to the Roger Dare. These would no doubt emerge as the course got under way.

Over the next two weeks, they were subjected to a barrage of exercises, workshops, and long sessions before mirrors, exploring facial expressions. "You are the raw material it is our task to shape," said Roger Dare, peering over shoulders into the mirror. "Your faces are the clay with which our potters will work."

David looked at his face. Then he looked at a photograph of Peter Finch. The eyes were different – that was the issue. Peter Finch's eyes were eloquent – that was the word – while David felt that his own eyes . . . Or was it the jaw? Was his jaw strong enough to convey determination – when determination was called for? Or was it more suited to an impression of hesitation, or even weakness?

"You can do special exercises," Henry said, when David spoke to him on the subject. "They develop the chin muscles. Do you know that your chin has muscles?

But I wouldn't worry too much – your jaw is pretty average, I'd say, which means that its well suited to lots of parts."

David looked at Henry. His face was nothing special; in fact, it was one of those faces that was instantly forgettable. If you saw Henry on the street or on the tram, five minutes later you would never be able to recollect what he looked like and give a description. All that you could say, David thought, was "eighteen-ish, average height". Even the colour of his hair was indeterminate. It could be called dark, but then, in a certain light, it looked much fairer. And some of it was short, while in other parts it seemed to be fairly long.

He wondered whether Henry was doing the right thing in hoping to go on stage. And he detected a similar reservation in the way in which Roger Dare and some of the other staff members looked at Henry when he was doing the prescribed exercises. Roger Dare was careful not to single out any one student for praise or criticism, but when he watched Henry he almost always frowned, as if puzzled about something.

"I'm finding this course really tough," Henry confided in David at the end of the first month. "I'm working at it as hard as I can, but I don't seem to get anywhere. Yesterday, in play reading, I stumbled over every line – every single line. I couldn't get it right."

"Nervous?" asked David. "Maybe you're too nervous."

"Maybe. I tell myself not to worry, but . . ." He shrugged.

"Have you tried breathing exercises?" asked David. "You take a deep breath, and then you hold it in. It calms you."

Henry was keen to clutch at any straw. "Does it work?"

"It does for me," replied David. "Sometimes I get a bit jumpy just before I go on. That's when I take a deep breath and hold it in. It works for me."

The following day, the class was divided into small groups to work on short excerpts from well-known plays. Henry and David were both in a group allocated to a scene from *The Importance of Being Earnest*. Virginia was in this group and was revelling in the role of Lady Bracknell.

"Suits her," whispered David.

"Stuck-up tart," Henry whispered back.

But Henry was nervous – David could tell that as he glanced at his friend. His hands were shaking, and his breathing seemed shallow.

"Take a deep breath," David said out of the side of his mouth. "Then hold it in for as long as you can. Really hold it. Your heart rate will go down."

Henry did as David suggested. Inhaling deeply, he closed his eyes and clenched his fists. Virginia noticed this.

"What's with him?" she asked.

David gave her a discouraging scowl.

And then, after a rather short time, Henry fainted, falling heavily to the floor, like a puppet whose strings had suddenly been cut.

"Jeez!" exclaimed Virginia.

Roger Dare was standing nearby, his empty cigarette holder protruding beneath his nicotine-stained moustache. He spun round, saw Henry, and rushed to his side. The cigarette holder fell to the ground and broke in two pieces. Seeing this, Roger seemed to forget for a few moments about Henry and busied himself in retrieving the broken holder. That left it to David to attend to the casualty, who by now had come round and was trying to sit up.

Roger Dare bent down to examine Henry. "You all right, my dear fellow?"

Henry made little of what had happened. "I'm just fine. I passed out, I suppose."

"He was holding his breath to calm his nerves," explained David.

Virginia overheard this. She laughed. David spun round. "What's so funny?" he spat.

"Keep your hair on," said Virginia.

Roger Dare asserted his authority. He glanced disapprovingly at Virginia. "You go and sit down, Henry," he said. "If you need to go home, that's fine. Take the day off."

Henry retired to the side of the hall, from where he watched the others performing Wilde. Afterwards, he and David went for lunch in the café down the road from the drama school.

"I'm sorry I suggested that breathing thing," said David.

"You weren't to know, mate."

"Yes, but still . . ."

Henry sighed. "I shouldn't have fainted. That's another thing I'm going to have to work on – not fainting."

They treated themselves to a large pizza and talked about the lives they had led before coming to Melbourne.

"I've been thinking," said Henry. "Both of us have families who wanted us to be something other than what we wanted. Do you think all families are like that?"

"Not all," said David. "Some, but not all."

Henry sighed. "I don't think I'm ever going to get anywhere with acting. I don't know if I've got the talent."

David was quick to disagree. "You've got heaps of talent, Henry. Heaps. It'll come. All you have to do is loosen up."

"And not faint?"

"That too."

Henry looked wistful. "Do you really think I've got talent?"

David nodded. "Yes, I do."

"And Virginia?" asked Henry.

David had to admit that he thought Virginia would probably be a success. "People like that usually are," he said. "I know it's unjust. I know that it shouldn't happen – but it does."

"So, there's no fairness in life?" said Henry. "Is that what you're saying?"

David lowered his eyes. "Something like that," he said.

After a few months in Melbourne, Henry acquired a girlfriend. He had met her at a party held by a cousin of his, an engineering student at the university. She was called Penny and was the daughter of a successful car salesman, Ern Throwover. The unusual name had become well known in Melbourne from the stickers that his cars bore on the rear window, each proclaiming, *Another Great Car from Throwover Motors.* Penny had recently celebrated her twentieth birthday, being six months older than Henry, whom she called, for some unexplained reason, Hoggy. She had an open, rather optimistic-looking face, with a slightly retroussé nose around which was a scattering of faint freckles. Henry told David that he had counted these freckles, and that the total was thirty-four. "There's one that I'm not sure about," he said, "so I didn't count it. If it becomes more definite, I'll make it thirty-five."

As befitted the daughter of Ern Throwover, Penny had a car of her own, a pastel-coloured French sedan with her father's sticker loyally displayed on the rear window. Most of the students at Roger Dare could not afford cars and were envious of the few who had one. Virginia, in particular, made scathing references within Henry's hearing to the "very odd-looking, vomit-coloured car" from which "somebody" – she did not name him – was occasionally dropped off for classes. This brought amused glances directed towards Henry, who pretended not to have heard but noted these remarks with a mixture of embarrassment and cold anger.

Virginia eventually met Penny in a nearby café where she found her having lunch with Henry. Uninvited, she joined them at their table and took the opportunity to find out more about the other young woman. Henry felt deeply uncomfortable; he could see that Virginia was assessing Penny, trying to elicit her views on a variety of subjects and even asking her about "that lovely car" that she had occasionally seen her in. Unaware of the undercurrent of animosity, Penny spoke freely, telling Virginia about an overseas trip she had been taken on the previous year in which she had been to Rome and Venice and also to Copenhagen. "I really liked Sweden," she said.

Virginia smiled. "Yes," she said. "Great place."

"Have you been there?" asked Penny.

Virginia glanced at Henry. She shook her head. "No, but I do know where it is."

Henry swallowed hard. "Copenhagen's . . ."

He left the sentence unfinished. He wanted to correct Penny, but he felt it would only make it worse. He was already imagining what Virginia would say to the others. "She thought Copenhagen was in Sweden – she really did. I'm not making this up. True as God. That girl is *really* stupid."

He mentioned the encounter to David later that day. "She was leading Penny on," he said. "She was trying to make her look stupid."

David listened gravely. The problem, he thought, was that on this occasion, Virginia was right. Penny was not very bright. There was no way round that brute fact. She knew nothing – or next to nothing – and was slow to pick up on most things. This was not to say that she did not have her good points – she was kind and supportive, and she made Henry feel good about himself. That was more important than anything else.

"Penny's not stupid," said David. "Far from it."

Henry looked at him appreciatively. "She knows quite a lot," he said. "It's just that she doesn't show off – know what I mean?"

"Yes," said David. "Unlike some people. Unlike Her Flaming Highness, Virginia."

They both laughed.

Nell took to Henry the first time she met him.

"I like your friend," she said, after David had brought Henry back to the house one Saturday afternoon. "I like people who are straightforward."

"I like him too," said David. "We seem to be on the same wavelength."

Nell nodded. "Wavelengths are the thing, aren't they? And you know immediately if you're going to be able to communicate with somebody. There are some people who are just . . . well, just impossible. Hopeless. No shared values."

David thought of Virginia. She was an example.

"And you think it's pointless trying to get anywhere with people like that?" he asked.

Nell thought about this. "Probably. You may get through a little – I'm not saying that you can say *nothing* to them, but it's an uphill battle. And most of the time, I think it's hardly worth it." She paused. "Jimmy Gordon next door – his wife, Barbie. You haven't met her yet, but she's an example. She and I are never going to agree about anything. She's National Party – goes to all their meetings. Makes the sandwiches. But while I could forgive her that, she's anti-everything remotely modern. Hates modern art. Sees reds under every bed. Doesn't like artistic men. It's a long list. She's impossible – no two ways about it. She should go and live with the bogans in Dandenong."

She suggested to David that he invite Henry to dinner at the house one Sunday. "You tell me he has a girlfriend," she said. "He could bring her, if he wishes. What's her name?"

"She's called Penny," replied David. "Penny Throwover."

Nell frowned. "The car people?"

"That's her dad."

"They're both invited," said Nell. "I'll get a rack of lamb."

Henry and Penny arrived in the pastel-coloured car. David came out to greet them at the fleur-de-lys gate and brought them in along the shell-lined path.

"Are those real shells?" asked Penny.

"Concrete," David replied.

"Fabulous," said Penny.

Henry pointed to the wooden sign on which the house name was displayed in burned lettering. "Montmartre," he said.

"What's that?" asked Penny.

"It's a part of Paris," David explained. "Artists live there. And there are nightclubs."

Henry put a hand on Penny's shoulder. "Penny's been to Paris."

"I know," said David. "I want to go some day. God, I want to get away."

"From here?" asked Penny. "Don't you like it here? Fitzroy North?"

"From Australia," said David. "Not permanently. Just for a while."

"When you're a famous actor," said Henry, "you'll be living in London. Or even New York. We'll come and see you."

Penny gave Henry a sideways glance. David thought she blushed. "We?" she said.

"You can come too," muttered Henry, embarrassed.

David saw Henry look down at his feet. They had reached the small porch at the front of the house. David felt a rush of affection for him. Not only was he physically clumsy but his friend's awkwardness extended to saying the wrong things, too. David wanted to say to him that it didn't matter; that he was who he was, and that he liked him in spite of it, and that it was obvious that Penny liked him too – and Nell. He was a good bloke. That could compensate for just about anything: that you were a good bloke.

Nell served their dinner, which they ate outside, on a table that she had set out in the back garden. They ate early, and at the beginning, as they supped at the chilled white wine Nell had brought for the occasion, there was still some sun that shone through the wine glasses, refracting coloured light onto the tablecloth. Then the sun went down, and Nell brought out four candles, which she placed in the middle of the table. Stars swung up in the sky – and the Southern Cross was high above them.

Nell asked Henry whether he had ever acted in a Shakespeare play. "David tells me he played Lear," she said.

Henry replied that he had been the understudy for Richard Gloucester in an abbreviated version of *Richard III* they had performed at school. "Somebody else played Richard," he said. "But they let me be the understudy."

"What's that?" asked Penny.

"It's the guy who learns the part in case the main actor gets crook," explained David. "All the big theatres use understudies. If Hamlet gets run over by a tram on his way to the theatre—"

"Or he loses his voice," interjected Henry. "Then the understudy comes on."

Penny looked disbelieving. "He just sits and waits?"

"Yes," said Henry. "I didn't have to go on stage."

"It must be unusual for a school production to bother with understudies," said Nell.

There was a silence. David knew why Henry had been an understudy. It had been the consolation prize, as he would never have been good enough to take the principal role. He looked away, in case Henry should see that he knew. But Henry now said, "I think they asked me to be the understudy because they didn't think I was good enough to be in the play but they still wanted to give me a part."

"Nonsense," said David. But he said it too quickly.

"Why would they do that?" asked Penny. "You're a great actor, Henry. Everybody says that."

David laughed. "He's better than I am – I can tell you that." And he added, "And I'm not going to get very far, as it happens."

Nell admonished them both. "You boys just need to have confidence. You both have it in you. Of course you do. Why else would you be at drama school?"

"Yes," chimed in Penny. "Why else?"

Nell started to rise from her chair. "I've got Shakespeare in there."

"In the house?" asked David.

"Yes. In my bedroom. All the plays. Ten volumes. They belonged to my mother. I love Shakespeare." She was looking at Henry. "If I get it, would you read something from *Richard III*?"

Henry gave a nervous laugh. "Right now? Me?"

"Yes," said Nell.

She made her way into the house. Penny giggled. She turned to Henry. "I'd like to hear you, Hoggy."

"I'm not very good," protested Henry.

"Nell would like it," said David. "We don't get much Shakespeare round here. Do it for her."

Nell returned, carrying a large, blue-bound book. She had inserted a marker, and now she opened it at the chosen page and handed it to Henry.

"There's a very moving speech there," he said. "Poor

Richard. It's where Shakespeare reminds us to feel sorry for him."

"Why?" asked Penny.

"Because he wasn't very nice," said Nell. "I don't know what they teach you in history these days, but I learned about him when I was at school."

David avoided looking at Penny. He doubted if she knew much history.

"He was accused of killing his nephews," Nell continued. "He smothered them with a pillow while they were staying in the Tower of London."

Penny looked surprised. "He was their uncle?"

"Yes," said Nell.

Penny shook her head. "Some uncle," she said. "I don't think I like the sound of him."

"There are those who say that he was innocent," said Nell.

"Then why did he kill them, if he was innocent?" asked Penny. "That doesn't make sense to me."

David looked at her. He had never been sure what Henry saw in her – apart from the obvious. That was the trouble with the obvious – it tended to obscure the not-so-obvious. Nell was also looking at Penny and smiling. "History can be really interesting," she said.

The remark was not addressed to anybody in particular, but it was Penny who replied. "I really like history," she said. "There's so much of it. All that stuff."

Nell pointed to the book. "Go on, Henry," she said. "Give us Richard's speech."

Henry stood up and started to read the speech.

David closed his eyes. He was cross with Nell, because he thought she should not be embarrassing Henry in this way. He was her guest, and you did not ask your guest to read excerpts from *Richard III* unless you were confident that they wanted to do it. And poor Henry – look at him – he was so wooden in his delivery.

At the end of the performance, Penny stood up and kissed Henry before he could sit down.

"That's phenomenal," she said.

Henry sat down. He was pleased with how he had done, and now he glanced at David for confirmation.

"That was terrific," David said. "It's a great piece of theatre, that." He paused. "Should we tell Mr Dare about that? Should we suggest he chooses it for one of our classes?"

Nell remembered something. "I saw Roger Dare in Shakespeare once. I'd forgotten that, but now I remember. He was playing . . . I can't recall, actually, what it was, but it was here in Melbourne. There was a big piece about it in *The Age*. I remember they said it was odd that he should have had a cigarette holder in his mouth when playing Coriolanus."

"Did Coriolanus smoke?" asked Penny.

Henry shook his head.

"Who knows?" said David.

Nell was tactful. "I don't think tobacco existed in those days." She laughed. "It's one of those things most people – including myself – don't really know about, isn't it? When did people start smoking? I'm not sure."

Penny said, "I don't know. Sorry."

David now mentioned that Roger Dare had repaired his cigarette holder with a piece of sticking plaster. "He dropped it when . . ." He stopped himself.

"When what?" asked Penny.

David looked apologetic. "When Henry fell over."

Penny looked concerned. "Did you fall over?"

"I fainted," said Henry. "I was holding my breath, and I fainted. I was out of it for only a couple of seconds."

"You mustn't hold your breath," said Penny. "Okay? Don't hold your breath."

"I won't," said Henry, and he took her hand and pressed it.

"Good," said Nell. "Thanks for reading that, Henry. You did it really well. I felt I was there, right there, watching Richard."

"Did he die in real life?" asked Penny.

"Everybody dies in real life," remarked David, and laughed. Nell looked slightly pained. She gave Penny a protective look; at David, she glanced reproachfully.

They sat outside for half an hour longer. The stars were bright. The sound of laughter drifted across the fence; others were sitting out on this warm night, under the stars. A car went past in the road; a dog barked, briefly, before a shout silenced it. David felt happy. He was with his friends. He was doing what he had always wanted to do – he was in the theatre. He had his life before him. He had no reason to be anything but content.

The course lasted a full year. At the end, a small graduation ceremony was held in the practice hall. Students were invited to bring friends and family to listen to Roger Dare making a speech and presenting the graduates with what he called a "certificate of successful completion".

"When you graduate from a university," he said, "you get a few letters after your name. Of course, if you are a successful actor, you don't need anything like that. My friend David Niven used to say that he did very well without the letters B.A. after his name – and I think he was right. What counts is what's in the box, not the label. Peter Finch, a great actor – whom I am proud to be able to call my friend – he says much the same thing. But you people who are graduating today from Roger Dare do have some letters after your name, and I'll tell you what they are: S.U.C.C.E.S.S. For those of you who don't have your dictionary with you, that spells 'success'. Your road to success starts today, as you leave this academy. Put you heart into the theatre, and the theatre will put its heart into you. That's what you need to remember when you leave this place."

David invited his parents and Nell. They sat proudly in the front row, listening appreciatively to Roger Dare's speech.

"So, he knows David Niven," whispered David's mother. "You heard that? David Niven. The one who was in *Separate Tables*. Remember?"

"It shows," his father replied, *sotto voce*. "This bloke's got class."

At the reception following the ceremony, Roger

Dare made a point of chatting to every guest, posing for photographs with parents and family friends, his cigarette holder in hand, a fresh sticking plaster around the break. Nell reminded him that she had seen him as Coriolanus, and he put a hand to his brow in astonishment. "Such a long time ago," he said. "So much water has flowed under the bridge since then."

"I enjoyed it very much," said Nell.

"Darling, you're too kind," said Roger Dare.

Virginia sought out David at the end, just as the guests were leaving.

"I'm going to miss you and Henry," she said. She looked in Henry's direction; he was with his parents and Penny on the other side of the room. There was pity in her glance.

"I'm sure we'll all see one another around," said David.

Virginia nodded. "Poor Henry," she said. "I doubt if he's going to get any work. He's so *sincere*, if you know what I mean, but I don't think he really gets it."

David stiffened. "What's *it*?" he asked.

"Acting," replied Virginia airily. "You get it. I hope I get it. Most of the others get it. But not Henry, I'm afraid."

She looked at David, as if challenging him to disagree. But he was silent. There was no point in engaging with her, he thought; she would never change. You could say what you liked to her, but it would never make any difference.

"Did I tell you I've got a part?" Virginia asked.

David felt himself grow cold inside. "No, you didn't." He would not ask her what it was; he *would not*.

"Since you ask," Virginia continued, "it's theatre work. A four-week run – minimum, probably more. And the director has promised me something for afterwards, but I'm not sure if I'll take it. I'm interested in production, you know."

David bit his lip. I hate her, he thought. But then he thought, No, I don't. You shouldn't hate other people, Nell said, because it was just too exhausting. If people who hated other people put the same amount of energy into liking them, then they would find out that they didn't hate them at all. David wondered whether that was true. He could start, perhaps, by trying to like Virginia.

"I'm really pleased for you," he said. The words seemed to hurt his throat, and for a moment it seemed to him that he might choke.

"Are you all right?" asked Virginia.

"Yes," said David. And then added, "You must be very pleased. I don't think anybody else has got anything."

"It's early days," said Virginia generously. "Some of you may get something. You know what Roger says: persist. That's his motto, you know. He showed me this shield-thing he has on the wall. It has *Persto* painted on it. That's 'I persist' in Latin, you see."

David managed a thin smile. "'Presto' would be a good motto," he said. "If you were the impatient type, that is."

Virginia looked blank. Then she said, "Be that as it may."

Roger Dare came over to join them. "My star pupils," he said. "You and you. Star quality. Both going far."

He smiled at Virginia. Then he turned to David. "Have you got anything fixed up? Anything short term?"

David shook his head.

"Are you interested in something to keep the wolf from the door? *Pro tem*, of course."

"I'll do anything," said David.

Roger Dare seemed pleased. "That's the spirit. Take a job, I always say, and go to every audition you can. Audition, audition, audition. We all did that, and it's still the way to do it – unless you're lucky, like Virginia here, and walk straight into a major role."

"I owe it all to you," said Virginia.

Roger Dare acknowledged the compliment with a brief movement of his cigarette holder. "I do my best by all of you. It's all part of the Roger Dare ethos." He patted David's forearm, "And you, my dear fellow: I shall see you immediately afterwards – in the office. I'll give you the details."

He went off.

Virginia looked at David. "Creepy," she said.

"They're all like that," said David. "Theatre people are like that. It doesn't mean anything."

Within a short time, the reception was over. Nell was hosting a lunch for David's parents back at Montmartre, and she left with them; David said he would join them after he had spoken to Roger Dare. "He has a job possibility for me," he said. "I don't know what it is, but I'll find out."

"That was quick," said his father.

David was cautious. "We'll see what he says."

He waved goodbye to them and made his way to Roger Dare's office. The door was open, and he was beckoned in.

"Graduations are such bittersweet occasions," Roger Dare said. "They are a beginning, in a sense, but they are also goodbyes to some of the best friends you'll ever make – the very best friends."

"I've enjoyed myself here, Mr Dare," said David.

"I'm glad. And I've enjoyed teaching you – all of you."

David waited. Then he said, "You said you might need me for a job." David knew he did not want to go back home and thought it might help his cause to appeal to Roger Dare's sympathetic side, so he added, "I like the city. I like living here."

"Of course you do," said Roger Dare. "I come from a small town myself. A long time ago, of course, but . . ." He sighed. "Sometimes in my dreams I'm back there, you know. It's really depressing. I'm back in Mildura. I know it's not so bad these days, but when we lived there . . ."

"Dreams are like that, aren't they?" said David. "I sometimes dream I'm back at school. I have to write an exam and I know nothing about the subject – nothing."

"Too true," said Roger Dare. "Or you're at a party in your pyjamas."

A short silence ensued. Then Roger Dare said, "A friend of mine can give you a job. Not acting, I'm afraid, but it will keep you going. You can get time off for auditions. He's a theatre-goer – you'll find him to be a supportive boss." He paused. "Interested?"

"Could be," said David. And then, more enthusiastically, "In fact, yes, definitely."

"Good," said Roger Dare. "He said he'll train you on the job."

"And the job itself . . . ?" David began.

"Restaurant work," said Roger Dare quickly. "Waitering. The pay's not bad and the tips can be quite good."

David said nothing. It was as if a prophecy had come to pass. It was a Nostradamus moment.

For the next four years, David worked at the George Court, an expensive restaurant in the business quarter. The proprietor, Roger Dare's friend, was called Terence Collins. He had moved to Melbourne from Adelaide after selling the family hotel he ran there. When he first bought it, the George Court was rarely full, having been run down by its former owner. Terence Collins changed that, employing a chef who had built up a considerable reputation in Sydney but who had married into an Italian family in Melbourne and wanted to move closer to an ailing mother-in-law. This chef soon made his mark on Melbourne, and in due course was offered a daytime cooking programme on local television. This programme, *The Secrets of the Kitchen*, proved wildly popular, largely through the fascination the audience developed for the chef's colourful banter with the assistants who appeared with him on the show.

David did not mind being a waiter, and he was, in fact, rather good at the job. To add to the authenticity of the dining experience, he affected a French accent when speaking to the diners and would indulge in lengthy descriptions of the dishes on offer, using his hands to make extravagant and over-stated accompanying gestures. It was not uncommon for reviews of the restaurant to make particular mention of the "amusing and loquacious French waiter" who added considerably to the pleasure of visiting the restaurant. Terence Collins was pleased. "You bring them in, David. No two doubts about that, mate: you bring them in."

As Roger Dare had promised, Terence Collins was prepared to give David time off to attend auditions. These took place every ten days or so and could involve absence for an entire shift. Terence did not dock his pay, but encouraged him, even when audition after audition failed to produce any work.

At least there were occasional appearances in television advertisements, and these were lucrative enough to help David put down the deposit on a small flat not far from Nell's house in Fitzroy North. Nell wanted to help him with this purchase, even though she knew that she would miss him terribly when he moved out. "He's the son I never had," she confided in a friend. "But one has to let go."

"True," remarked the friend. "Plenty of people have let me go in my lifetime."

Nell still had faith in David's acting ability. "Remember," she said, "even if things are slow right now, remember that you played Lear. Don't forget that. And remember what Roger Dare said about you. He said you could be a star. He said that, David. I heard him. Those were his very words."

David shrugged. "Something may turn up. Who knows?"

"You can come round here for meals any time," said Nell. "My door is always open – you know that."

He looked at her fondly. Melbourne was full of people like Nell – decent people, generous people. It might be a bit stuffy at times, but decency trumped stuffiness, he thought, and he had decided that he would not mind too much if he ended up living in Melbourne for the rest of his life. He was realistic now about the chances of ever reaching the West End in London, or Broadway, or anything like that; he would make do with whatever came his way, even if it was only the occasional part in local repertory theatre. And if he could get more television advertisement work, that would help him save towards the overseas trip that he would like to make at some point. He had always wanted to see Paris. He could visit the real Montmartre and send a postcard back to Nell saying, *Recognise the name of this place?* He would try to get to Rome too. As a boy he had been given a book called *Ancient Rome for Boys and Girls* that had a large picture of Christians facing the lions in the Colosseum. At the age of seven that had led to some confusion when he had heard mention on the ABC News of the Coliseum Theatre in Sydney. Were there really lions there, and did that sort of thing still happen, right here in Australia? He thought of the local Anglican vicar, who had a scar on his left cheek. Had that been inflicted by a lion? Had the Reverend Jones succeeded in getting away, perhaps by leaping from the stage of the Sydney Coliseum before the lions could pin him down? Now he remembered his quaint childhood misconception, but the thought of seeing the Colosseum, or what remained of it, still appealed.

He moved into his new flat. He was proud of it and chose his furniture carefully. Nell gave him an armchair, an occasional table, and a mattress. Henry gave him a radio, a bathroom cabinet he had been planning to throw out, and a wine-rack capable of holding a dozen bottles.

It was through Henry that David met Annie Harkness. She was a radiographer, and she was friendly with Henry's sister, who worked in the Melbourne children's hospital. David met her at a party that Henry held, and he and Annie took to one another immediately. Six months later they were engaged, and they married four months after that. David's flat was their first matrimonial home, and Annie set out to make it as comfortable as possible. She disposed of Henry's wine-rack and bathroom cabinet, but kept the chair, table, and mattress that Nell had donated. When the batteries in Henry's radio failed, she threw that out too.

Annie was vaguely embarrassed that David made

his living as a waiter. "Don't get me wrong," she said, "there's nothing wrong with being a waiter, but don't you think you could get something a bit more . . ." She searched for the word but could not find it.

"Prestigious?" suggested David.

"I wasn't thinking of that," she said. "It's just that you could get something that used your mind a bit more – know what I mean?'

David smiled. "I do use my mind," he said. "Every day. You try remembering what eight people want for their main course. You try remembering that this person can't take vinegar on his salad, or that person wants carrots but no broccoli, and so on. You try remembering what the six specials are and how chef has cooked them."

She apologised. "I didn't mean to be rude, David. Sorry. It's just that . . ."

"And at least being a waiter gives me the time to go to auditions. A lot of auditions are in the morning, and I don't work then – or at least, not before twelve. If I had an office job, I couldn't keep going off for these."

"You're right," she said. "And the important thing is your acting career, David. I know how much that means to you."

"So, I'll just carry on at the restaurant for the time being," he said. "Something may turn up."

"It will," said Annie. "It will, David. I know it will."

Annie was right. It did, and it turned up in the restaurant, one Friday afternoon, when Roger Dare made a reservation for a table for three. David took the telephone booking.

"My dear fellow," said Roger. "How nice to hear your voice. I take it that all is well?"

"Just fine, Mr Dare. Just fine."

"Splendid. I wonder if you could keep a table for three – one of those nice ones by the window. I'm going to be lunching with an absolutely charming chap who might – just might – have something for you. But enough of that. The lips are sealed – sealed tight – until we see one another at the appointed hour."

David was intrigued, but Friday was a busy day in the restaurant, and he did not have the time to think about what Roger Dare had said. In due course, though, his old tutor arrived, and David took him and his two companions to the best table in the house.

"Just the place," enthused Roger. And then, turning to one of his friends, a mild-looking man wearing horn-rimmed spectacles, he introduced him to David. "This is Tim," he said. "Tim is . . . now, wait for it, roll drums, tra-la, a . . . famous television producer."

Tim looked embarrassed. "Not famous."

"But, my dear fellow," said Roger Dare, "you have such a long list of successes appended to your humble name. You mustn't be so modest."

"I don't know," said Tim, glancing at David as he spoke. "I've got a lot to be modest about."

David smiled. He could tell that the glance Tim had given him was one of appraisal. He hoped that there would be no misunderstandings. He seated them and then went off to fetch the martinis they had ordered. As he left the table, he felt Tim's eyes on him.

He returned and passed them each their martini.

"A martini at lunch on Friday," said Roger Dare, raising his glass in a toast. "How much more sophisticated does it get, I ask myself."

Then Tim reached out to touch David's sleeve.

"Roger says you're one of his graduates."

David nodded. "Yes. I enjoyed the course very much."

Once again, Tim's eyes went up and down him. David felt even more uncomfortable. He was aware now that he was blushing.

Tim now turned to Roger. "You're right," he said. "He's the type."

Then, to David, he said, "Would you mind repeating after me, 'I've had a bad day at work. I can't take any more, Helen. I just can't.'"

David did as he was asked.

"Nice," said Tim. "Now, would you mind saying, 'You say that one more time, Eric, and I'll tell Helen everything you think I don't know. I'm warning you.'"

David caught Roger Dare's eye. Roger nodded his encouragement.

Right, thought David. I shall over-act. The lines were hardly poetry, but David delivered them with all the resonance and power of the Shakespearean stage.

After David had delivered his line, Tim clapped his hands together. "A natural, Roger. You were spot on. This is Bruce, as I live and breathe. Perfect. Right looks, right voice. Everything."

Now he addressed David. "You've just had an audition, David. An unusual one, yes, but an audition nonetheless."

"Tell him," Roger urged.

Tim turned round in his seat so that he was speaking directly to David. "We're about to start filming a new soap right here in Melbourne. Good budget. Six months airing guaranteed, whatever the figures are – although they'll be good, I can tell you." He paused. "I'm casting. And I think you're just right for one of the principal characters. He's called Bruce, and I had in mind somebody who looked just like you and who spoke very much as you speak. Interested?"

Federation Street proved to be wildly popular. David's character, Bruce, was not the lead, but was nonetheless important to the story, and appeared in just about every one of the three episodes made and broadcast each week. It was demanding work, even if playing Bruce came naturally to David: the hours were long, and the script could change with very little notice. But the atmosphere on the set was always friendly, and the fees increased as each season attracted a wider and wider audience. David now found himself being smiled at in the street and frequently stopped for his autograph by some die-hard fan. Now he went back to the George Court as a diner, taking members of the cast as his guests, and was fussed over by the waiters – other resting actors – who all knew of the extraordinary stroke of luck that had propelled David from obscurity to soap stardom. They hoped that a similar thing might happen to them, but knew it was unlikely.

"Lightning doesn't strike in the same restaurant twice," said one of the waiters, another Roger Dare graduate. "But you never know."

"No," said David. "The important thing is not to give up hope."

It seemed that *Federation Street* would run indefinitely. David was friendly with the principal screenwriter, a man called Maurice, a television veteran who had another five years to go before retirement. "As far as I'm concerned, Bruce is safe for five years, mate," said Maurice. "I'm not going to write him out. You happy with that?"

"Sure," said David. "Suits me. I like the part."

David had now been in the series for five years, and a further five years would bring his involvement up to a full decade. There were few actors who enjoyed that sort of continuity of employment. "I'm really lucky," he said to Annie. "This has been our big break, you know."

"You're wonderful," she said. "Everybody loves Bruce. You make him so . . . so human."

David smiled. "Long may it last," he said. "And as far as I can see, it will."

David was in the bath one morning when the call came in from Roger Dare. As he stood in the corridor, a towel wrapped about him, he could tell immediately from Roger's voice that something serious had happened.

"My dear fellow," Roger began, "I have the most terrible news to give you. Horrible news. Dear Tim has been taken from us."

David waited, his heart suddenly a cold stone within him. He struggled to speak. "What . . . what happened?"

"He and Caroline went up to Queensland on one of these short breaks."

"He mentioned he was going," said David. A plane crash?

"He went up north – the Daintree, I believe. And he went fishing."

David held his breath.

"A beastly crocodile took him," Roger went on. "I don't have all the details, but apparently he was trying to release a trapped line and he fell into the water. The salty was waiting."

David said nothing.

"You there, my dear fellow?"

"Yes. It's . . ."

"It's awful. Indescribably awful."

He and Roger spoke for a few minutes longer before Roger hung up. David went into the kitchen, where Annie was making scrambled eggs. "Tim," he said. "A crocodile got him."

Annie gasped. David sat down. They stared at one another, uncertain what to say or think.

Tim was replaced by Virginia. Since her graduation from the Roger Dare, her career had taken her to Sydney and, for a period of three years, to London. Now she had returned to Australia and was contacted by a head-hunter to see if she would take over the production of *Federation Street*. She had agreed, provided that she was allowed to do some direction as well. These terms were agreed. She would be principal producer and, at the same time, she would direct half of the episodes.

Virginia addressed the cast and crew on her first day in the job.

"I know how much you people are missing Tim," she said. "He was one of the greats. But I'm sure that he would want us to carry on much as before. That will be his monument – a smooth transition into a new era for *Federation Street*."

Taking David aside, she said to him, "It's great seeing you here, David. Just like the old days at Roger Dare's."

"It's great seeing you, Virginia."

"And tell me, how's Henry?"

David explained that Henry had had a few parts here and there.

"Back half of a pantomime horse?" asked Virginia, and then laughed.

David bit his tongue. He had to work with this woman.

"Poor Henry," said Virginia. "And that girlfriend of his? Miss Einstein? What was her real name?"

"Penny. He married her."

Virginia rolled her eyes. "Oh well," she said. Her tone changed. Now she was sympathetic. "I do hope he's happy. I suppose one comes to terms with . . . with one's lot in life. Poor Henry. Such a pity."

They got down to work and, over the next few months, none of the actors noticed any difference in their working lives. But then at the end of a full day's shooting, Maurice came up to David and whispered, "You and I need to meet in the pub right now."

David asked him if there was anything bothering him, but Maurice seemed unwilling to speak. "In the pub," he said. "Half an hour's time – okay?"

Maurice was already there when David arrived. The screenwriter nodded to him and took a sip of his beer. "Bad news," he said. "We had a storyline meeting this morning. Me, the story editors, and Virginia."

David knew what was coming.

"I'm out?"

Maurice nodded sadly. "Afraid so. I argued against it, but Virginia wasn't listening. She said . . ." He hesitated, but David urged him to continue.

"She said that she thought you had become stale. She said we need new blood."

David was aghast. "Stale? But . . . but look at the audience figures. And the letters we get. Nobody else thinks that."

Maurice shrugged. "She does. And she wants to replace Bruce with a new character, Tony. He's going to be Hazel's ex-lover who's come back from Hong Kong and wants to set up a gym and personal trainer's business. He was in the series back in the day.

A really flat storyline, if you ask me. But that's what she wants."

"And me?"

"You're going to be taken by a crocodile on a trip up north."

David stared at Maurice with disbelief. "That's really tactless," he said. "After what happened to poor Tim."

Maurice agreed. "That's what I said, but she just laughed and said that if that sort of thing could happen in real life, then it could happen in a soap." He paused. "And there's more. You remember who played Tony when he was in the story before? He's going to play him again. Same actor. Jack Porter. Yes, him. And you something else? Who is Virginia's long-term lover, in real life? That's right. Jack Porter. They've been shacked up for years."

It took David a few moments to absorb the full perfidy of the plan. The budget restricted the number of actors who Virginia could employ. If she wanted to give a job to her actor lover, then she would have to get rid of an existing member of the cast – and that, it transpired, was to be him.

"I hate her," David muttered. "I try not to hate people – I really do. But I hate her, I'm afraid."

Maurice nodded. "You're right about hate, Dave. It never helps. But sometimes it's understandable."

David looked down into his beer. He did not feel like drinking.

"When?" he said.

"It's going to be done in stages," replied Maurice.

"Jack is going to be introduced next week. We'll be filming with him. Then the following week you go to Queensland and you're out. She'll probably be telling you that tomorrow. She said something about it. She's planning to get rid of Bill as well."

"Bill!" David exclaimed. Bill was the popular and long-serving principal cameraman. Like Maurice, he was getting into his late fifties and might not find it easy to get another job.

"Who's going to take Bill's place?" David asked.

"Jack's cousin," replied Maurice. "He was with the ABC up in Darwin. He's left them and is looking for something down here. I heard from one of the technical people that it was all stitched up."

David sat back in his chair. He and Annie had recently bought a new house. The repayments were large. They would manage, but it would be tough.

"Sorry about this, mate," said Maurice. "I thought you should know." He looked at David apologetically. "I'm going to have to write the relevant episodes tomorrow and the day afterwards. We're shooting them on Friday. I'm not looking forward to it."

Later that evening, David and Annie went out to dinner at Henry and Penny's house. David told them about what he had just learned from Maurice. Henry listened with a growing look of disgust on his face.

"Ghastly woman," he said.

"I remember her," said Penny. "She made me feel this small." She made a gap between her thumb and forefinger.

Henry shook his head. "It's so unfair. You're so popular. The viewers love you."

"They do," said Penny. "The woman in the pharmacy told me that you're the reason why she watches *Federation Street*. She said her sister-in-law agrees with her."

"They all love you," said Henry. "Penny's right."

"You need to fight back," said Penny.

David made a despairing gesture. "I don't see how I can. The producer runs the show. Virginia calls the shots – that's just the way it is." David's eyes suddenly widened. "Unless . . ."

They looked at him.

"Unless what?" asked Henry.

"Unless what was meant to happen to Bruce were to happen to Tony – he's the ex who has turned up from Hong Kong."

Henry frowned. "I don't get it."

David explained. "Unless the crocodile gets Tony rather than Bruce."

"It's all the same to crocodiles," interjected Penny. "We all probably taste much the same to them."

Henry smiled. "You'd taste really good," he said to Penny. "I'd be a bit tough."

"No, you wouldn't," Penny replied. "You'd taste just right, Hoggy. No, I'm serious – you would."

Annie steered the conversation back to David's suggestion. "Tell us what you have in mind," she said.

David told them, and they listened carefully. At the end, Henry voiced his doubts. "It all depends on whether the technical people – the people who do the transmission – are prepared to play ball."

"Yes," said David. "It does. But I can tell you something: there are one or two of them who are no friends of Virginia's. It's old business – I don't know what it is, but there's feeling there."

"In that case," said Henry, "you could try. I take it that Maurice would be on board."

David explained that he was confident that Maurice would be only too happy to be involved. "He realises that Virginia is behaving corruptly. There's no other word for it. It's corruption. Maurice is dead straight. He doesn't approve of that sort of thing."

"Good," said Henry. "Then do it."

Maurice required no persuasion.

"Brilliant plan," he said. "But let's just go over it again. I write the episodes that Virginia wants. All as ordered. Yes?"

"Yes. Then in the lunch-hour, when nobody's around, we record an alternative episode. Virginia's always away on a Wednesday afternoon, so she won't find out. In this episode, Tony goes to Queensland and the news comes through that he's been taken by a crocodile. We obviously can't let him in on this, and so it will all be done through reportage. But he'll definitely be written out."

"And you stay in?"

"Yes. Then we give that version – the one we've made ourselves – to the technical people and get them to transmit it instead of the official one, so to speak.

It goes out in the evening – in the usual slot – and viewers throughout the country see it. As far as they are concerned, that's Tony out of the story while I remain in."

Maurice chuckled. "And she won't be able to do anything about it, as you can hardly reverse what has already been broadcast."

"Exactly. And at the same time, we go to management and put our cards on the table. We tell them about how she's proposing to replace Bill with her cameraman cousin. They won't like that."

"And I tell them that if nothing is done about it, I'm out of it and they'll not get a replacement in time."

"Yes," said David. "Then we hope they fire her."

"I normally don't like getting people fired," said Maurice. "But there are occasions where it is the only right and proper thing to do."

"We should always behave correctly," said David.

"In life and in drama," agreed Maurice. "Oh, this is very satisfying."

"Revenge can be like that," said David. "As long as it's calibrated correctly."

"And is it? In this case?"

"Absolutely."

It worked beautifully. The unofficial episode was recorded at a time when the only people in the studio were the conspirators. Then it was handed over to the technicians, who took the official recording off the system and substituted the version in which Tony meets with an untimely end in Queensland. That episode was then transmitted.

Virginia called a meeting to establish what had happened. When David saw her, she was shaking with rage. He said, "Your little game's over, I'm afraid."

Her lower lip trembled. There were little flecks of spittle on it. "My little game? What do you mean?"

"We've discussed it with management, Virginia. They were appalled. You're history. Sorry to be so blunt, but there we are. And poor Tony. Such a pity. That's not a nice way to go."

For a few moments, David thought that she might slap him. He saw her hand rising, but then it dropped, and she turned away.

As for *Federation Street*, it continued to prosper. Maurice seemed to acquire a new creative wind, and his plots became even more emotionally engaging and charmingly impossible. Viewer ratings climbed and climbed. Virginia was replaced as producer by Henry. That was David's suggestion, but it was one that was approved of by management, as the CEO of the company was a close friend of Henry's father, having been in the same masonic lodge for years. Penny was given a small part but proved to be so popular that she was promoted to a much more significant role.

The four of them – David, Annie, Henry, and Penny – went to dinner at Nell's house to celebrate the fact that everything had worked out so well. Nell said, "I'm so proud of you, David – I really am."

Nell had barbecued lamb chops. She had made a

special potato salad to go with the chops: this involved mustard seeds and chopped chives. They ate outside. There was a suggestion of a breeze, just a suggestion, and it was like gentle breath against their skin, the gentle breath of the one you love. The Southern Cross hung in the sky, its points bright, confident, reassuring.

"I am so happy," muttered David.

"Yes," said Nell. "We all are."

CAVALLERIA RUSTICANA

An Introduction

In what follows, there is an act performed by one of the characters that, when looked at afterwards, seems appalling. Its potential effect is dreadful, and its effect on the actor is profound. Yet it is typical of the sort of human act that may be performed without having been thought through beforehand by the actor. Not everything we do is fully intentional. Not everything we do is accomplished after we have considered the consequences. Not everything we do is the result of what is sometimes called "joined-up thinking". We act in the dark, sometimes on impulse, unaware of the ripple effect of what we do. We may act in a particular way because we are responding to internal promptings for which we are not entirely responsible. Much of our action may even be determined by influences and events that occurred before we were born. To recognise that is not to commit oneself to a completely deterministic view of human action; it is simply to recognise the truth of the proposition that who we are and how we view the world may be determined by the bed in which we happen to be born, by the society in which we grow up, and by the beliefs with which we are endowed.

To give an example: the people who burned witches

in the seventeenth century did not do so because they were inherently evil people: they did what they did because of where and when they were born, and because of the beliefs they held as a result of those factors.

Judging the past by the standards of the present is facile. Some judgement is possible, but it must be tempered by an understanding of the historical context in which human action takes place. That is not to say that past wrongs should be presented as anything but wrongs: cruelty does not become something other than cruelty simply because it was perpetrated by those who felt they were not being cruel. What it does mean, though, is that we may have to recognise that the perpetrators of acts of cruelty or injustice may not have grasped the objective wrongness of their acts. The judicial torturer of the past may have considered himself an agent of justice, determined to elicit the truth, rather than a torturer. That may limit the usefulness of condemning him for what he did.

Then there is the notion of accident. At one level what happens in this story is simply an accident. That is debateable, and yet we must be very careful to preserve the notion of accident as an exculpatory category. People should not be held responsible for that which they do by accident; only if an accident flows as a direct and foreseeable result of a freely chosen action should an accidental consequence be laid at the door of an actor. If, when approaching a road junction, I genuinely fail to see an approaching car, and if, at the time, I am driving with due care and attention, I do not see how the collision that follows can be seen as a result for which I can be held *morally* accountable. That is the whole point of the word "accident": an accident is an event that is nobody's fault. Unfortunately, we live in days when we are particularly keen to find somebody to blame for any misfortune that occurs. We want scapegoats, even if they are innocent. This is dangerous, as it has the effect of making society retributive and morally undiscriminating. It leads to harsh judgements and the pillorying of those who meant no harm. To live in a world in which morally nuanced assessments of human acts is impossible because the public wants blood . . . That would be a nightmare – but it is a nightmare to which we might be closer than we think.

I feel sorry for everybody in this story. I feel sorry for the person who exacts revenge, because, on balance, revenge is wrong and never helps. I feel sorry for the dog, because he is a dog, and should be judged as a dog. Dogs bark: it's what they do.

MONTY, TIGER, ROSE, ETC.

Rose first saw Colin at the thirtieth birthday party of her vivacious, redhead friend, Vicky. It was a large party, held in Edinburgh, at Vicky's father's golf club. "Vicky has *countless* friends," somebody once said to Rose. "It's something to do with being a redhead. You speak to virtually anybody – *anybody* – and they'll say, 'Oh yes, I know Vicky.' One hundred per cent of the time. Try it."

So, it was not surprising that when Vicky decided to have a party to celebrate her birthday – "Almost a third of a century!" she remarked – there were over sixty people there. And that was just the tip of the iceberg, people said. Those were just the close friends – there were plenty of others who heard about the party and who would have loved to have been there but who were not invited. "You just can't keep everybody happy," Vicky said.

But Rose, who turned thirty the same year, was there because she had been at school with Vicky, and they were like this, she said, crossing two fingers to demonstrate the closeness of their friendship. And because they were so close, Rose felt she could be frank with Vicky about her interest in Colin, as they looked across the crowded room at the well-built man near the window. "I'm going to faint, Vicky. Seriously. Faint. Look at him – I mean, just look at him. Where did you get him? A male-order catalogue?" She paused, then spelled out the word "male".

Vicky laughed. "That's an idea," she said. "They could have one of these catalogues with the models wearing the sports shirts and chinos and so on, but you can't order the clothes – you order the man himself. A great idea."

Rose waited. "So?" she prompted.

"All right," said Vicky. "He's called Colin. Colin Fanshaw. Lovely name, that, don't you think – Fanshaw." She paused, and then continued, "I wouldn't, if I were you."

Rose looked puzzled. "You're warning me off?" It occurred to her that Vicky might be involved with Colin, in which case she would apologise for her tactlessness and bow out – it was Vicky's party, after all.

Vicky lowered her voice. "Colin is good-looking – *very* good-looking, but" – she lowered her voice even further – "he's also very dull."

Rose cast a glance across the room to where Colin was standing in a small group. They were all laughing. He did not look dull to her. "He doesn't look—"

Vicky cut her short. "But he is. He's perfectly nice, but . . . do you want a man to be *that* nice?"

Rose looked thoughtful. Her last boyfriend, Freddie,

from whom she had recently parted after two years, had been possessive and demanding. A nice man, she thought, was just what was required. "I've got nothing against nice men," she said.

Vicky shrugged. "Do you want to be introduced?"

Rose hesitated. She could not see any reason why she should not at least meet Colin. If he proved to be as dull as Vicky suggested, then she could easily detach herself and talk to somebody else. There were plenty of ways of getting away from bores at parties. "Yes," she said. "If you don't mind."

Vicky smiled. "Poor Colin," she said. "He means well. He's an accountant, by the way. I think he does tax returns – that sort of thing." She gave Rose a knowing look. She had given her every warning and need not reproach herself. Some women, of course, liked dull men and, for all she knew, Rose was one of them. There was no accounting for taste, she thought, as she led her friend across the room, through the throng of partygoers, her friends, all celebrating her birthday, all well disposed towards her.

Rose whispered to her, "I was just interested in meeting him – that's all."

Vicky laughed. "Your secret's safe with me."

Rose blushed. It had always seemed to her to be most unfair that an overt expression of interest by a woman in a man was taken by some – not all, of course, but certainly by some – to be something to feel apologetic about. It was yet another example of the double standards that people had in these matters. Things were changing, of course, but not fast enough, in her view.

They reached Colin and his two friends. He turned to face them. "The birthday girl," he exclaimed, holding his arms out towards Vicky. "Come and give Colin a big kiss."

Their first date was to a cinema. The film was not one that Rose was keen to see as she had read a very lukewarm review – "What's this film about?" asked the reviewer – but Colin had chosen it and she had gone along with the suggestion. He had called her after she had given him her telephone number at the party. "What about a movie?" he had said. "The Dominion Cinema? Any time that suits you."

She hesitated, but only for a few moments. Vicky had been right, she thought: Colin was not very exciting. But at the same time, there was nothing exactly *wrong* with him. He had been good-looking when seen from over the other side of the room, and he had been even more so when viewed from close-up. But were looks enough to sustain a relationship? Marrying for looks was as pointless, she said to herself, as marrying for money. But then she stopped herself. Was marrying for money pointless, or was it simply *expedient*? There were many people who married for money and never regretted it – not for one, sybaritic moment. She knew at least one person who had married a much older man who happened to be extremely wealthy. He had lasted two years and then died. "So considerate of him," another friend had observed. He had left her with two expensive flats, a house in France, and a forty-seven-foot yacht in an Ionian marina. The widow had dyed her hair and started a new life. "She turned quite blonde with grief," observed the same friend.

Colin arranged to meet Rose at the cinema, where he bought two tickets for the large sofa seats at the back. Then he went off for two large tubs of popcorn. She did not like popcorn, but she tackled it nonetheless. Colin said, "This is great, don't you think? Sitting here, eating popcorn. Just great."

She said, "Yes. I like the cinema."

"I'm glad," he said. "I've always liked the cinema – ever since I was a boy. There's something about it, you see – I don't know what it is, but there's something about it."

She thought about this, and then replied, "It's dark, I suppose."

"And there are films."

"Yes, the films are important."

The advertisements began. She glanced at him in the semi-darkness. His profile was really breathtaking, she thought. He was like one of those Greek gods with their straight noses descending like a mountain ridge. And she thought, There's nothing wrong with being handsome. Sometimes, good-looking people could be pleased with themselves; often they could be narcissistic, and arrogant too. But then there were people who had those sorts of looks and yet were modest and unassuming. She felt that Colin was probably one of these, and this realisation made her warm to him.

They went out for dinner later that week. Then he invited her to an office party. "They're mostly tax accountants," he said. "But they're a great crowd, you know."

At the party, one of his colleagues said to her, "So you're the Rose whom Colin's been talking about. He said you were a real stunner. And I see what he means."

She felt flustered. The tone of the remark was intrusive – the colleague was a flirt, she thought – and yet it pleased her to hear that Colin felt that way about her. Her fondness for him increased, and she decided that the following week she would mention him to her mother. She had said nothing yet, as she discouraged her mother's only too obvious desire to interfere in her private life, but now she thought the time was right to say something.

Rose's parents lived in a part of Edinburgh that had views of the Firth of Forth and to Fife on the other side. Rose had been brought up there, and her parents still kept her bedroom exactly the way it had been when she had lived there. It was at the top of the house, under a combed ceiling; and if you craned you neck when you looked out of the window, you could see the islands of the Forth, indistinct blue shapes in the distance.

Her mother, Elaine, chaired four committees. She played bridge to a high standard and was a member of the official government body that supervised the ancient monuments of Scotland. She was tireless in her fundraising for charity and was a regular correspondent in the local newspaper, berating the government for its various failures. Rose was her only daughter, and Elaine was ambitious for her. When Rose was still at school, she had lined up various boys of her age whom she thought would, in due course, be acceptable suitors. Her favourite amongst these was a boy called Lawrence, whose father was a professor of medicine, and who, in Elaine's view, would be an ideal husband – in the fullness of time, of course. Lawrence, however, did not like girls, and he declined to dance with Rose, or anybody else for that matter, at the Edinburgh Teenage Ball at the Highland Show Grounds.

"I don't understand that boy," Elaine complained.

To Rose it was perfectly obvious. "I do," she muttered, keeping her voice down so that her mother would not hear her.

"You'd think he'd like to meet a few girls," Elaine continued.

"No, you wouldn't," said Rose, again *sotto voce*. You'd imagine that mothers would know about that sort of thing, Rose thought, but perhaps they did not.

Rose had gone to university – in Stirling – where she started a degree in business studies. That lasted five months, and then she decided that university was not for her. She accepted a job in Julie's Designs, a wedding dress shop on the south side of Edinburgh. It had its demanding moments, but she found that she enjoyed the work and the contact that it brought with people. She had been there for ten years now and had no desire to move.

"You need to get a qualification," her mother said. "What if you lost your job with these dress people? What would you be able to offer another employer?"

Rose shrugged. "I can do . . . general stuff."

Elaine stared at her. "General stuff? And what, may I ask, is general stuff?"

"It's stuff that needs doing," Rose replied. "That sort of stuff."

"Darling," sighed her mother, "fond though I am of you, at times you can be infuriating. The world is a very competitive place. You can't go through life thinking that 'general stuff', as you put it, will be there for you. A lot of 'general stuff' has been outsourced, for a start. There just isn't enough 'general stuff' to go round."

"I'll be all right," said Rose. "There are lots of things I can do."

Elaine struggled to control herself. She wanted to shake her daughter. She wanted to say to her: do you realise just how much you do *not* know about the world? But she knew that would be the wrong thing to do. You could not reason with so many of the young, because they were incapable of realising that they might be wrong. That was no fault of theirs, of course; it was simply the way that people of that age were. Neuroscience was always coming up with new insights into the folly of youth, showing us how the plasticity of the brain persisted until well into the twenties; and that until they reached maturity, people might be hard-wired to think in a particular way, or fail to see things that would be perfectly apparent to those a bit older than they were. One had to be tolerant. Rose would come round to her way of thinking, Elaine told herself; it was just a question of time.

Now, when Rose broached the subject of her new relationship, Elaine listened attentively, but tried not to give the impression of being too anxious about what she was being told. She was aware of her daughter's sensitivity over what she saw as unwarranted parental interference, and Elaine had learned to retrain herself. It did not always work, but at least she tried.

Elaine struggled to keep her voice even. "A new friend?"

"Yes," replied Rose. "He's called Colin."

"Colin?" Once again, Elaine battled to preserve the impression that she would never pass judgement on something as unimportant as a name. "Colin?" she repeated.

Rose pursed her lips before replying. Her mother was a snob: it was as simple as that. What was wrong with being called Colin? Did she think it was *common*? Throughout her childhood, that word had hovered around in the background. *Don't do that, dear, it's a bit common.* She actually said that sort of thing, Rose reminded herself. Her mother said that in the twenty-first century. It was ridiculous. The idea that anything could be disapproved of because everybody did it, was absurd. We were all common, when it came down to it. We all came from the same stock, ultimately – and nobody was inherently any better than anybody else. Surely everybody realised that by now – but not her mother, apparently.

"Yes," said Rose, engaging in her own struggle to keep the temperature low. Elaine was her mother, after all, and she still loved her, in spite of her attitudes. All mothers had attitudes, she thought, and sighed inwardly. They said things that were completely at odds with the way people felt these days. They were ambitious for their offspring. They thought their own children could do no wrong, even when other people's children were meeting with disapproval for one reason or another. Mothers! What could one do but sigh?

"Yes, Mother. Colin. You'll like him, I think."

Elaine tried to smile. "Oh, I'm sure I shall, Rose." And then she thought about Freddie, who had been the last one, Colin's predecessor. Whatever Colin's drawbacks might be – and they would, no doubt, be revealed in due course – he could hardly be worse than Freddie, with his discoloured teeth, and his going on and on about tennis. And then there was the fact that he had no prospects, or none that she could see, at least. He worked in a camera shop, and it was difficult to see where that would lead. Eventually, though, Rose had seen sense and decided that he was too controlling and possessive. Elaine could have told her that right at the beginning – it was obvious what sort of man Freddie was – but there would have been no point in trying. Everybody knew, Elaine told herself, that if you made your reservations too obvious, then that would simply encourage your son or daughter to dig in. Everybody knew that. So, Elaine had bitten her tongue time and time again, and said nothing.

Now it was different. Freddie had been shown the door and it would be possible to be more honest about how she had felt.

"I must say, Rose, that I'm sure Colin is an improvement. He must be."

Rose said nothing. She watched her mother.

"It's not that I didn't try with Freddie. You know that, I hope. Anybody you bring home is welcome here – of course they are. It's just that Freddie was a bit . . ."

"Common?"

Elaine affected surprise. "I'd never say that, Rose. Never."

Rose thought, You'd think it, Mother. But she did not say that. She said nothing.

"Freddie had his good points," Elaine continued, trying, as she spoke, to think of them, but concluding that there were none. "It's just that I thought – and Daddy, you know, thought the same, although he never said anything to you – I thought that you could do so much better." She paused. "Did you ever manage to get Freddie to go to see Mr Macgregor about his teeth?"

Mr Macgregor was the family dentist. He lived in a village just outside the city with his Polish wife, who bred poodles.

Rose looked resentful. "It wasn't for me, Mother. You don't tell other people to do things about their teeth. Teeth are a private matter."

"Oh, I don't think so, Rose. I don't think teeth are private at all. We all see each other's teeth, surely. And if somebody has halitosis, well . . ."

Rose glared resentfully at her mother. "Freddie did not have bad breath. He had a slight discolouration of his teeth because of . . . because of . . ."

Elaine waited. It was poor dental hygiene, in her mind, but she doubted if her daughter would see it that way.

". . . because of some mineral deficiency when he was a boy. That can cause discolouration in a person's teeth."

Elaine looked sceptical. "Mineral deficiency? In the water? If that were the case, then surely we'd all have discoloured teeth. We all drink the same water, after all."

She waited for her daughter to answer, but Rose was smarting in silence. Now her mother went on, "Of course, Freddie was from Glasgow, wasn't he?"

The silence continued, but now seemed even heavier.

"And they like their Irn-Bru over there, don't they?" Irn Bru was an orange-coloured, sugary drink, popular in the west of Scotland.

Rose shrugged.

"I imagine it's not terribly good for one's teeth," said Elaine. "But I don't know. I might be wrong about that."

Rose looked out of the window. It was a defence mechanism to which she often resorted when speaking to her mother. She took a deep breath and decided to ignore the comments about Glasgow and Irn-Bru. "I thought that I might bring Colin round," she said.

"That would be wonderful, darling. We'd love to meet him. And . . ."

"Yes?"

"And, Rose, I want you to know that we shall make every effort – *every* effort – to get on well with him. If you like him – and you must, I imagine – then that's enough for Daddy and me. We'll like him too."

Rose stopped gazing out of the window. "He's an accountant. Daddy can talk to him about that."

The effect of this disclosure was immediate – just as Rose had imagined it would be. "An accountant?"

"Yes, he's a partner in a firm of tax accountants. They have a branch in Glasgow too, and one in Aberdeen."

This was wonderful news – quite wonderful. "My goodness. They must be busy."

"Colin works in the Edinburgh office."

That was *very* acceptable. "Quite right."

"And he went to Watson's." Watson's was a large Edinburgh school of which Elaine approved.

"A very good school. Daddy almost went there, remember?"

Rose nodded. "I remember."

Everything had changed now, as far as Elaine was concerned. "We'd love to meet Colin. Invite him to dinner. Next week, perhaps. Would that suit you? And Colin too, of course. He must be very busy."

"I'll ask him."

Elaine moved towards her daughter. She put an arm on her shoulder. "We want you to be happy, darling. That's the only thing that counts – the only thing. Happiness. And if Colin makes you happy, then that makes Daddy and me happy too. You know that, don't you?"

Rose had to admit to herself that she knew that. And when the meeting took place the following Friday evening, she felt relief that her parents gave every sign of liking Colin. And this continued over the following weeks, when, for one reason or another, she and Colin paid several visits to the parental home.

It was after one of these visits that her father drew her aside.

"A word in your ear, Rose."

She waited.

"This is a slightly delicate matter," he began. "But I thought I might have a word with you about it, nonetheless. Your Colin . . . We do like him, you know. Mummy and I really get on with him, and she tells me that she thinks . . . Well, she thinks you might be serious about one another." He laughed. "I'm not one to pick up on these things, of course. Women's business. But if that's true, and if that means that you and Colin will be joining forces, so to speak, then I want you to know that I would like to transfer some funds to you to help buy a place."

He looked at her and smiled. She returned the smile – instinctively, warmly.

"Six hundred thousand pounds," he said.

She struggled to speak. But then she said, "Six hundred thousand?"

"Yes. I imagine that Colin will have access to the balance of what you'd need for a nice house. Somewhere like Balerno, for instance. Have you thought of Balerno? Or Currie?"

Balerno and Currie were two villages on the edge of Edinburgh. The houses were comfortable – and expensive. They had large gardens and a view of the Pentlands, the hills that rose to the south of Edinburgh. Balerno was aspirational – it was not first home territory.

But here was her generous father making it possible.

"Daddy, you're so kind. You're the kindest man in Scotland. You really are." She kissed him. Then she thought, I'll give him six kisses – one for each hundred thousand pounds.

He looked bashful. "Have I read the situation correctly?"

She nodded. She had been intending to tell them, but not just yet. Now, however, it seemed right to break the news. "Colin and I are getting engaged. I was going to tell you. And he wanted to have a word with you too."

Her father nodded. "The formalities, so to speak. And, of course, it has our blessing. I wouldn't be doing this if it didn't."

"I suppose not."

He became business-like. "Talk to Colin. Tell him what we have in mind. Then start looking for a suitable place."

She did as he suggested and spoke to Colin that evening. Colin shook his head in astonishment. "I had no idea your old man would be so generous," he said. "Amazing."

"He said we should start looking."

Colin said that his friend, Gavin, worked for one of the large estate agencies. "He has houses on his books that will be sold off-market. He knows what's out there."

"I can't wait," said Rose. "Our own place." She looked at Colin fondly. I am very lucky, she thought. I have a nice, easy man. He may not set the heather alight – there are certainly more *interesting* men around, but that's not what I want. I don't want to be married to the *Encyclopaedia Britannica*. I want to marry a man who will get on with things quietly; who'll fix things that go wrong in the house; who'll go off to the supermarket for me from time to time – and stick to the list; who'll let me do the things I want to do and not want to be in my hair all day. That sort of man. And Colin, she was sure, was that.

For his part, Colin was proud of Rose. She was attractive, and she did not sit around, as some women did, and expect to be fussed over. She was her own person. And part of that, of course, was her career, that was just about to take off. The owners of Julie's Designs had decided to retire, and they had offered Rose first refusal on the business. The shop was held on a lease, and so the asking price was purely for the goodwill. This proved not to be too expensive, and Colin was easily able to arrange the financing for Rose. He was proud of the fact that his fiancée was a managing director, even if the business of which she was managing director only employed one other person.

Gavin got in touch a few days later about a house that he thought might suit them. "It's in Balerno," he said. "Just off the West Lanark Road. There's a street of houses built about fifteen years ago. They're all high value, although some are a bit smaller than the one I have in mind for you."

Colin asked about the number of bedrooms and garages. Gavin replied that there were four bedrooms and three garages.

"Three garages?" exclaimed Colin. "Now you're talking, Gavin."

"I knew you'd like that," said Gavin. He turned to Rose and smiled. "Men's business, you see. Men like garages."

Rose laughed. "Sad," she said. "Poor men."

"And the garden is fantastic," Gavin went on. "I was looking at it the other day, when I was out there to get the particulars. Two acres, which is pretty good for somewhere so close to town. It needs a bit of work, but—"

Rose interrupted him. "That's fine by me," she said. "I've always wanted to have my own garden. I've been doing an online course in horticulture."

"She's very smart," Colin said to Gavin. "She knows what's what."

"I'm sure she does," said Gavin, inclining his head to Rose. "There are plenty of possibilities with this garden. You wait and see. You'll be thrilled, I suspect."

They went with Gavin to inspect the house. The owners were out, but Gavin had keys, and he led them through each room, pointing out features that he thought might interest them. "Of course, you have to see beyond the present owners' taste," he said, looking askance at a set of curtains in lurid lime-green. "But once you do that, you see the potential."

Rose agreed. She glanced at Colin and sensed that he shared her enthusiasm for the house. While Gavin went off to deal with a phone call, she and Colin conferred privately. They both wanted the house.

Three months later, a matter of days after their wedding, they took possession of their new home. Colin was planning to convert one of the three garages into a workshop, while Rose immediately started work on the re-design of the garden. She ordered a large load of topsoil, with the intention of creating new beds, planting shrubs and trees, and a new rockery in which she would plant alpines. Elaine gave them a generous garden centre voucher, with which they decided to purchase a water feature and two garden benches. "I always thought you'd make a very good gardener," she said to Rose. "I always thought that."

Parts of the garden were already well established. In the vegetable section, there was a large bed of garlic that had been planted in January by the previous owners and was now full of healthy-looking plants. Rose was delighted by this: she loved garlic, and the thought of having her own crop was particularly appealing.

Rose was happy – perhaps happier than she had been for years. She had decided that she loved Colin, even if she had rapidly plumbed whatever depths he had – and these were hardly profound. He was undemanding company and utterly predictable in his attitudes and his habits. The adjective that best described him, she felt, was "inoffensive". And to that, she felt she might add "solid", "decent", and "reliable".

Elaine agreed with her daughter's assessment. Her relief at the wedding was palpable. Until the ring was placed on Rose's finger and the minister uttered the words that declared the couple husband and wife, she had been concerned that something might happen to frustrate the union. Somebody would change his or her mind – it happened, after all, and sometimes at the very last moment, right at the church door or altar. But now any change of mind would be too late: Rose had become Mrs Colin Fanshaw, and he had, by the same token, become Mr Rose Fanshaw. It was perfect, as far as Elaine was concerned, and her pleasure in this outcome was enhanced by the thought of what might have been had Rose married Freddie. There was a world of difference between being mother-in-law to a good-looking partner in a firm of accountants and being in the same relationship with a man with stained teeth who worked in a camera shop. The average life was littered with close shaves, she believed, and that was one of them.

"I thank my lucky stars that Rose chose Colin," Elaine confided to a friend. "When you think of what some parents get when it comes to sons-in-law, the blood runs cold."

"Ice cold," agreed her friend. "No known faults?"

Elaine shook her head. "Not as far as I know. He's not the most exciting man in Scotland, but who wants excitement?"

"Not me," said the friend, perhaps a bit wistfully.

Rose and Colin's house had a name: Pentland View. This was a reference to the Pentland Hills, which rolled out from the southern boundaries of Edinburgh; soft, feminine hills, unlike the higher mountains of northern Scotland. The name was appropriate, as the view from the house was, indeed, of the Pentlands and of the stretch of farmland between the city and the hills.

On either side of Pentland View were houses built at the same time, but of rather different style and, in both cases, slightly smaller. One of these houses was called Waverley, and the other was called Cairnside. Waverley was owned by a retired couple who spent much of their time away, at a country cottage in the Scottish Borders, near Selkirk, not far from Abbotsford, the home of Sir Walter Scott, author of the *Waverley* novels. That provided the key to the house's name. Rose and Colin met this couple on the day they moved in, when the husband brought over a bowl of home-grown strawberries as a welcome gift.

"This is a very friendly community," he said. "We've been happy here, and I'm sure you will be too."

Rose asked about Cairnside, enquiring as to who lived there. Their neighbour hesitated. It was only a brief hesitation, but Rose noticed it.

"They're away at the moment," he said, glancing over the fence in the direction of the other house. "He's an engineer in the oil industry up in Aberdeen. He spends quite a bit of time on the oil rigs, I believe. And she . . ." There was a further hesitation, again a short one, but eloquent for all its brevity. "She calls herself Tiger." This was accompanied by a raised eyebrow. "I have no idea what her real name is. There's a husband called Ray, I believe."

Rose waited. Would more information be forthcoming?

The neighbour looked away. "We don't see a great deal of them," he said. And then he changed the subject. If she wanted help with the garden, he knew a man from Kirkliston who looked after gardens. He could put them in touch, if necessary.

"I'm planning to do the garden myself," said Rose. "But I'll let you know. Thanks."

The neighbour smiled. "It will be good to see this garden properly looked after," he said. "The last people made an effort, but I think they were too busy. His business was taking off and he had to go down to London a lot. She had a sister who wasn't very well and needed a lot of help. They didn't have the time."

"I'm going to do my best," said Rose.

"Good," said the neighbour.

Rose and Colin had taken a week off to get everything sorted out in their new house. On the third day after they moved in, their other neighbours, the owners of Cairnside, turned into the drive and stopped in front of their garage door. Rose watched from her kitchen window, standing sufficiently far back so as not to be seen from outside. She had a clear view of the parked car and the people getting out of it.

She smiled as she saw Tiger alight from the passenger's seat. Now she knew why the neighbour had hesitated. Tiger was a brassy blonde. Her hair was piled up in a beehive style, popular in the nineteen sixties and seventies but seen less frequently since then. She wore a tight, hip-hugging dress in pinky-beige. She looked as if she was somewhere in her thirties – not much older than Rose herself.

But it was her husband who was the surprise. He was short and stocky and wearing a T-shirt that displayed the muscled torso beneath. Even from a distance, she could see that his upper arms, knotty with biceps, were heavily tattooed. "Popeye," she muttered, and smiled to herself.

More was to be revealed. Tiger now walked round to the back of the car and opened one of the rear doors. As she did so, a large dog pushed past her, almost knocking her from her feet, and began to career around the lawn. The muscular man shouted at the dog, which ignored him and tore round the side of the house, only to emerge a few moments later from the front, barking loudly. Above the sound of the barking, she heard Tiger shouting out the dog's name. "Monty! Monty!" The dog ignored her too.

Tiger and the man went inside. Rose sat in her kitchen and thought about what she had seen. These were not the neighbours she had imagined for herself in Balerno, which had a reputation for quiet respectability. Tiger did not look the part, and nor did her husband, with his Popeye arms and tattoos. Of course, I shouldn't jump to conclusions, she told herself. I must *not* become my mother. I must *not*. She is the last person I should turn into. And yet, she knew that people often became their parents. It was depressing, yes, but it was often true.

Half an hour later, when Rose was in her garden, surveying a bed where she was planning to plant shrubs, she noticed that her neighbours had emerged from the house. Ray was carrying a suitcase that he loaded into the car before turning to give Tiger a quick kiss on the cheek. Then he got into the car, started the engine, and reversed down the drive. As the car set off, Tiger stayed outside to wave before going back into the house. She did not see Rose watching. Rose wondered whether she should go over to introduce herself but decided against doing so. She would go tomorrow, she thought, as it was a Saturday and Colin would be able to accompany her.

But the meeting took place earlier than she had anticipated. She remained in the garden for fifteen minutes but when rain set in, she took refuge back in the house. It was at that point, though, that she heard a furious barking outside. Looking out of the kitchen window, she saw that the dog she had seen earlier on, Monty, had crossed over from the neighbouring garden and was standing at the foot of a tree in her backyard, barking at a squirrel that had scampered into the branches above.

Rose was not sure what to do. She had nothing against dogs in general, but this dog made her feel uneasy. It was large and clearly aggressive, a Rottweiler, or perhaps a mixture of Rottweiler and some other equally unpleasant breed. Rose shuddered: she had read in the newspaper a few days ago of an unprovoked attack by one of these large, aggressive dogs on a man in Glasgow. The victim had been lucky to escape with his life and had ended up being badly scarred by the mauling. She would certainly feel very uncomfortable if Monty were to make a habit of coming into her garden. There was a fence between the two properties, but it had not been maintained, and she had already noticed that there were several places where it would no real obstacle to a dog.

Suddenly Monty stopped barking, and Rose saw that Tiger had appeared. She went up to Monty, calling his name while admonishing him volubly. She had a leash with her, and she clipped this onto his collar at the same time as she happened to look up to see Rose staring at her through the kitchen window.

Tiger gave a friendly wave as Rose emerged from the house.

"Sorry about this," Tiger called out. "Monty is a naughty boy sometimes." She looked down at the dog, from whose jaws a tail of viscous saliva was dripping down. "Who's a naughty boy, then? Who ignores Mummy when she tells him not to chase squirrels?"

With Monty having been scolded, Tiger beamed at Rose. "I'm Tiger," she said. "I'm your new neighbour – or you're mine. Same thing, I suppose."

Rose introduced herself. Monty was looking at her, as if sizing her up. The saliva detached itself and fell to the ground.

"He dribbles," said Tiger. "These large breeds often do, don't they?"

Rose dragged her gaze away from Monty. There was something nasty about the dog, she thought. There was something menacing about his eyes.

"I've told him not chase squirrels," Tiger went on. "If you find him going after them, don't hesitate to tell him off. He knows that he shouldn't be doing it."

The two women looked at one another.

"I'm really glad you've moved in," Tiger said. "The previous people were a bit . . . well, not to put too fine a point on it, a bit stuck-up." She put a hand to her mouth and giggled, as if she realised that she had spoken out of turn. "I hope they weren't friends of yours."

Rose shook her head. "We didn't know them."

"Well, they thought of themselves as superior, if you ask me. What's the word? Condescending."

"Possibly," said Rose.

"Anyway," said Tiger. "They're gone, and I'm not going to miss them." She paused. "Was that your husband I saw earlier this morning? Going off in his car?"

Rose nodded. "Yes, Colin."

Tiger grinned. "Dishy," she said.

Rose was uncertain how to react. You did not say things like that about other people's husbands – you just did not. She shrugged. "He's my husband," she said.

"I meant the car," said Tiger, bursting out laughing. "Dishy car."

Rose was flustered. This woman was playing with her. She did not mean the car – it was perfectly obvious that she was referring to Colin. There was no such thing as a dishy car.

"And that was yours driving off earlier on?" asked Rose.

Tiger pulled at Monty's leash, to stop him sniffing at Rose's feet. "Yes," she said. "That's my Ray. He works up in Aberdeen. He often goes out to the North Sea rigs. He's a mud engineer."

"Oh yes?"

"Yes. They're the people in charge of pumping mud into the oil wells to bring the oil out. It's an important part of drilling for oil, but most people don't even know they exist. That's what Ray does."

"Fascinating," said Rose.

"You and Colin should come round for drinks some evening," said Tiger. "When Ray's back. Not that I always know when that will be."

Rose accepted the invitation. "That would be very nice."

Tiger glanced around the garden. "It looks as if you're going to transform this place," she said. "It's become a bit of a dump."

Rose smarted at the insult. She had seen Tiger's garden, admittedly only from her side of the fence, but she had not been impressed. "I hope we make an impression on it," said Rose. "But it can take a long time."

"London wasn't built in a day," said Tiger.

Rose frowned. "Rome," she said.

Tiger looked surprised. "What about Rome?"

"I think that it was Rome that wasn't built in a day."

Tiger pouted. "I didn't say it was."

"Of course not."

There was a brief silence. Then Tiger looked at her watch. "Monty needs his tea. I always feed him at this hour of day. They get used to a routine, you know. And these big dogs have a hearty appetite. You wouldn't believe how much dog food we get through in a week."

"I bet it's a lot."

"Seven kilos," said Tiger. "Seven kilos!"

Rose expressed surprise. What was the point, she wondered, in having an animal like that eating one out of house and home? A West Highland terrier would be a much more manageable proposition and less of a drain on the earth's resources. Of course, some people wanted to have a large, powerful dog. What she had seen of Ray suggested that he might be such a person, with his bulging muscles and tattoos. And Tiger herself, she imagined, would probably want a very masculine dog rather than a simpering lapdog. It all made sense, perhaps.

Tiger suddenly asked, "You don't have a cat, do you?"

Rose replied that they did not. She liked cats, though, and had had a Burmese as a girl.

"Just as well you don't have one now," said Tiger. "It's a bit of a relief, actually, because Monty, I'm afraid, is not good with cats."

Rose looked down at Monty, who looked back up at her, his eyes filled with malevolence.

"Yes," Tiger continued. "The people in your house before you . . . What were their names again? The people who sold you the house?"

"They were called Drummond, I think."

"Yes, Drummond. Well, they had a cat – a very fat cat with one eye. I don't know what happened, but this cat had only one eye. This meant that he couldn't see as well as other cats."

"I can imagine."

"Anyway, he was also rather slow because he was so fat. It was their fault, I'm pretty sure. They fed him too much. He was always eating. And Monty, unfortunately, got him when he was outside and couldn't get to a tree in time. It was awful, but I don't think he felt very much. It was very quick."

Rose looked down at Monty again. It seemed to her that he was grinning with pride now. Impossible. He could not understand what was being said.

"They were really unpleasant about it," Tiger continued. "I didn't order Monty to do it. It's not as if I set him on the cat. The cat should not have been out on the lawn like that, especially since he only had one eye. What did he expect?"

Rose felt that she had to defend the cat. "I'm not sure. It was his garden, after all."

"But animals don't see it that way," protested Tiger. "Animals don't understand about human boundaries. How can they?"

"But animals do understand these things," Rose corrected her. "Animals are very territorial. They have a very clear idea of who owns what."

Tiger did not attempt to refute this, but she looked vaguely sulky.

"Anyway," said Rose, "I mustn't keep Monty from his food."

"No," said Tiger. "Monty can get very cross if we don't feed him on time." She looked down at Monty. "Who can be a very impatient boy? That's right, Monty, it's you that Mummy's talking about. Very impatient."

Rose resisted the temptation to call Colin at his office. She could not wait to describe Tiger to him, but she wondered whether she would be able to do her new neighbour justice. *London wasn't built in a day . . . It's you that Mummy's talking about . . .* And the beehive hairstyle. Everything. It was all terribly funny. And yet, at the same time, that dog was not at all funny. That was an evil creature, as all those fighting dogs were. It should be illegal to keep dogs like that – in fact, some breeds were already illegal, she thought, although it must be difficult to decide what dogs fitted into which category. Siamese fighting dogs, she thought; no, it was Siamese fighting fish. She smiled at the confusion: perhaps it was illegal to keep piranhas. Pit bull terriers? Was it against the law to keep a pit bull terrier?

When Colin came back from the office, she opened the front door to him with a grin on her face.

"I met our new neighbour," she said.

Colin put down his briefcase. "I need a drink," he said. "I've had a hellish day."

"Poor darling. Did you hear what I said?"

"No. Something about the neighbours." He took off his jacket and tossed it onto a chair. "Oh yes? Which one?"

Rose pointed in the direction of Tiger's house. "That one. And she really is actually called Tiger. Can you believe it?"

Colin smiled. "Is that really her name?"

Rose said that it was the way she had introduced herself. "And it suits her – it really does. She has a beehive hair-do – blonde, of course. Lots of curves. Make-up caked on."

Colin shrugged. "That's what these places are like. Move to Balerno and that's what you get."

Rose shook her head. "I don't think so. She's really . . ." She hesitated. She had no word for it, and she could not use her mother's term. She was not going to say that.

"Common?" said Colin. "That's what your mother would say, isn't it?"

Rose looked reproachful. "Mummy is old-fashioned. She doesn't see anything wrong saying things like that."

"I wasn't criticising her," Colin reassured her. And, he thought, it will take a lot for me to criticise any parents who give us six hundred thousand pounds.

Rose grinned. There was a certain pleasure in being on the side of the fallen angels – or at least on the side of the old-fashioned ones. "Actually, that's exactly what she is. Brassy as Sammy Burns' scrap metal yard."

"Hah!"

"I didn't meet her man," Rose continued. "I saw him. He looks like Popeye the Sailor Man, but a bit rougher. He's called Ray. He's gone off to do his mud engineering up in Aberdeen."

"Mud engineering?"

Rose gave the explanation that Tiger had given her. "They use mud to force the oil up. Apparently, that's what they do."

"Sounds messy," said Colin. "Not for me."

"But I did meet their dog," Rose said. "A horrible

creature. A Rottweiler crossed with something nasty – heaven knows what. Evil little eyes. Big jaws. Slobbering all the time."

Colin made a face. "Not very nice."

"No. He came over into our garden and chased a squirrel up a tree. Then she came back and started fussing over him like a mother hen. It was ghastly. Sick-making."

Colin opened the drinks cupboard that they had placed temporarily in the sitting room. He poured himself a whisky.

"I take it that we're not going to be close friends," he said.

"Definitely not," said Rose.

"Should we even try?" asked Colin.

Rose shook her head.

"Oh well," Colin said. "We could plant a hedge. A big one." He looked out of the window, into the garden. "And a fence. With a watchtower, perhaps. What do they say about fences?"

"Good fences make good neighbours."

"Yes. That." He looked at her, smiling wearily. "We don't need this, do we?"

She sighed. "You know what's been worrying me? It's the thought – just a possibility, of course – that the reason why the Drummonds moved is because of . . ." She inclined her head in the direction of Cairnside. "Because of them. Tiger and Ray."

"And the dog . . ."

"Yes, and Monty."

Colin looked thoughtful. "I don't blame the dog. Bad dogs are the way they are because of their owners. Good owners make good dogs."

Rose was not so sure. "Maybe sometimes," she said. "Then you get dogs that are just naturally bad – you know, it's in their genes. A form of canine original sin. Or canine psychopathy. Even if those dogs have good owners, their real nature will come out."

Colin conceded that this was true. But then he said, "Let's not talk about it any longer. Let's go out for dinner."

There was a restaurant just down the road – a place called The Hearth. Colin had suggested trying it when they had driven past it a couple of days earlier. Now he said that it would be a good way of de-stressing, and Rose agreed.

"I'm going to have a shower," he said. "And get out of this suit. One of these days, you know, men are going to revolt against suits. They're going to burn them and—"

His radical declaration got no further, as he was interrupted by a raucous barking from next door. This persisted, in spite of the sound of Tiger shouting, "Monty! Monty! Shut your face, Monty! I'm going to kill you, Monty!"

Colin glanced at Rose. She looked away. It was just too painful.

They returned from their meal at The Hearth. They had not been disappointed: the cooking was excellent, Rose said, and Colin got on well with the proprietor, Tony, who supported the same football team as he did, Hearts. They had a long chat about football while Colin was paying the bill.

"We're going to have a great season ahead of us with that new striker," Tony said.

"He was expensive," Colin said. "I hope he's worth it."

"Oh, he will be," Tony assured him. "You know what I always say? I say that every penny a team spends on a good player comes back doubled. Yes, that's true. You look at what happened to Celtic when they spent all that money on that Brazilian. Was it worth it? It most certainly was. You saw it with that goal in Amsterdam. Remember that?"

Colin did not. "I don't remember other people's goals," he said. "Just ours."

"Wise policy," said Tony. "Didn't T.S. Eliot say that people cannot bear too much reality?"

Colin looked puzzled. "Perhaps," he said. Then he added, "Not really. I've never heard that, actually."

"Well, he said something of that nature," Tony continued. "It was in one of his poems."

Rose smiled. "Colin doesn't do poetry," she said.

Colin looked at her. His expression was slightly cross – almost wounded. "And you don't either," he muttered.

Tony looked embarrassed. "Oh well, lots of people have said lots of things."

They travelled back in silence. As they neared the

house, Rose said, "I'm sorry, Colin. I'm sorry about what I said about you and poetry. I didn't mean to belittle you."

"Fine," muttered Colin.

"It's just that I'm feeling upset about things. My nerves are all frayed."

He slowed down. "About things? What things?"

"The new house. That dog. Is this how it's going to be? Are we going to have that creature barking his head off all day and night. And what if he attacks us?"

Colin attempted to make light of her suggestion. "He's not going to attack us. A lot of those dogs are all bark and no bite."

"I'm not so sure . . ."

They had reached their gateway. They had left it open. "And anyway," Colin said as he drove up the short drive to the house. "And anyway, if he did, we'd go to the police. They put down dogs that attack people."

"All very well when we're already being mauled," Rose said. "Not much comfort there."

"It won't happen," said Colin.

That night they were awoken shortly before midnight by a loud howling. Rose woke first and sat bolt upright in bed, her heart thudding. Then, still half asleep, Colin dragged himself out of bed and took a confused step towards the door. Rose switched on the light.

"That dog," she said. "What's happening?"

Colin crossed the room to the window and peered through the curtains. An outside light had come on next door, and he was able to make out the shape of the dog standing on the kitchen doorstep. The animal was quiet now, but after a few seconds he raised his head and howled again.

"He's shut out," said Colin. "She's put him out."

No sooner had he said this when a light appeared in Tiger's kitchen, and she appeared at the door.

"Bad Monty!" she scolded. "Bad, bad Monty!"

The dog scrambled into the house and the light was soon switched off.

"I don't believe it," said Colin. "She must have put him out deliberately. She must have known he'd make a commotion."

Rose lay back in bed. She reached over to the bedside lamp and switched it off. She could not think of anything to say.

It was not only the garden of Pentland View that required attention but the house itself. Although the roof was sound, there were tiles here and there that had loosened, and guttering that had blocked. There was something wrong with the water supply, too – a fault that had not been picked up by the surveyor in his pre-purchase report – and there had also been a call from the local council to say that a trench would have to be dug along one side of the property. And other small jobs needed to be done, with the result that there was a constant stream of tradesmen over the first three weeks of their occupation of the house. Rose took time off from Julie's Designs to deal with all this; she had a competent assistant there who was eager to show that she could run the business single-handed, if necessary.

The workmen from the council arrived that Monday morning. Colin had just left for work when they rang the doorbell and invited Rose to see where they proposed to dig their trench.

"It'll be a wee bit messy," said the foreman apologetically. "The water main here is deeper than elsewhere, but we'll try not to disrupt things too much."

The trench was dug quickly, a large mound of earth appearing on either side of the yawning gap in the earth. Rose took the three workmen a cup of tea at mid-morning and saw that they had excavated to a depth of ten feet or so. They told her that they had already installed the new section of pipe, but, since their mechanical digger had been taken off to another job, they would have to return on another day to fill the trench in.

Once they had gone, she spent several hours working on her new flower-beds and then an hour or two unpacking possessions that were still stored in the removal men's crates. She heard Monty barking from time to time and, on each occasion, she felt anger rise within her. There was no excuse, in her view. A large noisy dog was simply out of place in a suburb; he should be on a farm somewhere, not here where he was a constant irritant to neighbours, not to say a danger.

The next day, Elaine came to visit. She had seen the house briefly shortly after it had been bought but had not been back since Rose and Colin had moved in with their furniture. Now she stood in front of the house and cast her eye about the garden. Turning to Rose, she said, "There's work to be done, isn't there? But it's going to be worth it, I think."

Rose took her round to the back of the house to show her the work she had already done on the incipient vegetable patch. "Artichokes," she said to her mother. "See?"

"Watch them," said Elaine. "They spread."

"And garlic," said Rose. "That bed over there is entirely garlic. We shall be able to keep you and Daddy in garlic too. For the whole year."

"Good," said Elaine. "To have assured supplies of garlic is so . . . so reassuring, I always say."

They left the vegetable garden and began to walk towards the back door. As they did so, the sound of barking came from the other side of the house.

"A dog?" said Elaine.

Rose took a deep breath. "That's next door's. It sounds as if he's come in again."

Elaine looked concerned. "You'll have to nip that in the bud, dear. You can't have a dog running wild."

Rose felt irritated. She knew that. She felt that her mother assumed that she was somehow tolerating Monty. "I'm fully aware of that, Mother," she muttered through clenched teeth. "I haven't been encouraging him."

"You need to throw something at him," said Elaine. "Dogs soon get the message if you throw something at them."

"He's a very large dog," said Rose. "I'm not sure that would be wise."

The barking seemed to get louder, and a few moments later Monty bounded into view round the side of the house. When he saw Rose and Elaine standing stock still, staring at him, he stopped in his tracks. He sniffed at the air and growled.

"Shoo!" hissed Rose. "Go home, Monty. Shoo!"

Monty stood his ground. His growling became, if anything, rather more menacing.

"I'm going to have to call the police," said Rose. "I'm going to go inside and call the police to tell them there's a dangerous dog on the loose."

Elaine shook her head. "The police won't do anything. They're grossly under-resourced. They won't lift a finger for this sort of thing." She paused. "We're going to have to do something ourselves."

And with that, she bent down and picked up a steel garden trowel she spotted in a garden trug near their feet.

"Mother," began Rose, reaching out to restrain Elaine. "Please, don't." But it was too late. Her mother had hurled the trowel at the dog – and had done so with remarkable accuracy. The garden implement hit him squarely on the nose, causing him to emit a yelp of pain.

"Horrid creature," shouted Elaine. "Vile animal."

Monty's reaction to the onslaught was to turn tail and make his way as fast as he could for his own yard, howling in indignation as he did so. His flight was witnessed by Tiger, who had watched the encounter through her kitchen window and now came rushing out to embrace her traumatised pet. Bending down to embrace Monty, she examined his snout for damage. The dog's skin had been broken, and several drops of bright red blood now spattered onto the frilly white blouse she was wearing.

Tiger bundled Monty into the kitchen before striding purposefully across her small patch of lawn to the boundary between the two gardens. From where she stood, she was able to shout out to Rose and Elaine as they stood, paralysed by embarrassment, at the back of Pentland View.

"I saw that," Tiger screamed. "I saw what you did to a defenceless dog."

This was too much for Elaine, who quickly recovered from the shock of being shouted at. "Defenceless?" she shouted back. "Excuse me! That dog's positively dangerous."

This seemed to whip Tiger to new heights of indignation. "Pick on something your own size, you old cow," she screamed.

Elaine opened her mouth as if to say something in response, but the insult was too great. She could not believe it. This was Edinburgh, or almost; this was broad daylight; this was actually happening. Her eyes were wide with shock.

Rose shook a finger in Tiger's direction. "That old cow's my mother," she said. "I'd prefer it if you didn't insult her – if you don't mind."

Elaine looked at her daughter in astonishment. Momentarily confused, Rose said, "No, I didn't mean it that way, Mummy. I didn't mean to say that you're a cow."

Tiger overheard this. She laughed and then turned to go back inside. Rose groaned. "I wish you hadn't done that," she whispered to her mother.

But Elaine was unrepentant. "Did you hear her?" she asked. "Did you hear the language?"

"I know," sighed Rose. "But still . . ."

Once inside, Elaine sat down to recover. "You're going to have to act decisively," she said, her voice faltering. "You're going to have to put up a proper fence – all the way along that side. As high as possible."

Rose nodded glumly. "I know, I know. But it'll cut off the view from that side. We won't see the hills."

"You can't have everything. Hills or . . . or that dreadful woman and that Cerberus."

"Cerberus?"

"He was the dog who guarded the Greek Underworld," Elaine said. "He had three heads."

"Monty has one."

"Metaphor, darling."

They sat for a moment in the silence of the kitchen. Then Elaine said, "Try to think of some deterrent. Don't they make things that scare dogs off? Electronic devices? I seem to recall that Mr Macgregor said something about having a cat scarer on his lawn."

"Mr Macgregor the dentist?" asked Rose.

"Yes. They live not far from here, you know." Elaine paused. "Why not ask him?"

Rose shrugged. "I don't really know him that well.

And I went to Colin's dentist last time. He knows him from the golf club."

"I could ask Mr Macgregor," Elaine offered. "I have an appointment next week, as it happens. I could have a word with him. He may even know those dreadful people – or know about them, should I say?"

They saw nothing of Tiger over the next few days. They heard Monty barking, though, and there was a brief incursion during which he ran round their lawn once or twice before retreating onto his own territory. On several occasions, though, they were woken at night by his barking, when some movement in the garden – the sly passage of a fox, perhaps – attracted his attention. These incidents had a bad effect on Colin, who had difficulty in getting back to sleep once he was woken up. And sleep deprivation made him tetchy, which in turn unsettled Rose. Balerno was meant to be peaceful; that was why they had moved there; that was why they had committed all that money – the entire six hundred thousand pounds, topped up by a burdensome mortgage – to purchase something that was proving an elusive dream. It would have been more peaceful to stay in town, Rose thought – right in the middle of the city with all the noise that went with that, rather than to come out here to this . . . Rose searched for the right words, this . . . war zone. No, that was a bit extreme, Rose thought, but that was how it felt at times. The garden was the no-man's land into which forays had to be made under the watchful eyes of the enemy. At any time,

Monty might dash out like an enemy tank, every bit as threatening.

And then Monty dug up Rose's garlic. She was back at work now, and was about to drive off to Julie's Designs, when she decided to look at her vegetable garden. And that was when she saw the havoc wrought on her garlic bed, which looked as if a small earth-moving machine had moved through it. And the same thing had happened to a nearby flower-bed, where bulbs and plant stems were strewn in every direction. Rose looked on in utter dismay. There was no doubt in her mind that this was the work of Monty. They had heard him barking the previous night, and she had remarked to Colin that the barking seemed to come from their own garden. But they were half asleep and had done nothing about it – and now this was the result.

She summoned Colin to see the damage. He looked on in dismay. "Oh, darling – all that hard work of yours. All that work. That wretched dog."

Rose wiped at her eyes. "We'll have to get in touch with somebody about that fence," she said. She looked around the garden. It was a mess. Not only was there the damage that Monty had wrought, but the council had yet to return to fill in the trench. She had phoned them twice but had been unable to get beyond a recorded announcement proclaiming that her call was important to them. There had been no action.

Colin agreed about the fence. "I'll try to find a name," he said. "There'll be plenty of fence people."

It was that evening, though, that Mr Macgregor

called round, accompanied by his Polish wife, who bred poodles. He drove up in his blue estate car and knocked on the door while his wife remained in the vehicle.

"Mr Macgregor," said Rose, as she opened the door. "I didn't expect to see you. This is . . ."

"I was passing by," said the dentist. 'We live down at the end of the road, you know. I didn't realise that you had moved in until your mother mentioned it to me."

"Of course. She said she was going to be seeing you."

Mr Macgregor smiled. Rose noticed that he had very white, regular teeth. "Anna and I thought we should welcome you to the neighbourhood. You must meet Anna." He gestured towards the car.

"Won't you come in?" asked Rose. "Colin isn't back from work yet, but I can offer you coffee, perhaps."

Mr Macgregor shook his head. "We have to get back. Anna has her dogs, you see. Dinner time coming up."

"Of course. Poodles, somebody said."

Mr Macgregor nodded. "I call them Anna's nursery. She breeds them. Rather successfully, as it happens. Nice dogs." He lowered his voice. "I hear that you're having problems." He cast an eye in the direction of Cairnside. "Problems with certain people." He looked at Cairnside again.

Rose made a face. "I'm afraid so."

He lowered his voice further. "Dreadful people, I'm afraid. One doesn't like to be uncharitable, but . . ."

"It's their dog," said Rose.

"Oh, I can well believe it," said Mr Macgregor. "Your mother told me that the dog's been running riot in your garden. He attacked one of Anna's poodles, you know. We were in the village, outside the store, and that woman came along with her brute of a dog on a lead. Anna said that it lunged at her little Celia. It actually bit her around the neck. The vet had to put in six stiches."

They walked towards Mr Macgregor's car, from which Anna now emerged. The two women shook hands.

"This is a very nice house," said Anna. "You must be very happy to have found it."

"And a fine garden," said Mr Macgregor. He looked at the trench. "What are you doing over there?"

"The council," said Rose. "They dug it up to fix the water main. They're meant to be coming back to fill it in."

"They take their time," said Anna. "They always do."

Mr Macgregor smiled. He pointed to the trench. "It's a pity that their dog doesn't fall into the hole," he said. "That would give him a nasty fright. It would teach him a lesson."

Rose laughed. "Nice thought," she said.

"Your mother asked about electronic scarers," said Mr Macgregor. "You could try one, I suppose. We found that they can keep cats away, but . . ."

"But dogs don't seem to mind them so much," said Anna. "At least, that's been our experience."

"I'll look into it," said Rose.

"You must come and see us," said Anna. "I could ask

some of the neighbours for drinks. There are some very nice people round here."

"And some not so nice ones," said Mr Macgregor, with a grin.

Rose glanced at the trench. They were standing near it now, and it was deep and dark – to all intents and purposes, like a grave. She looked at Mr Macgregor. He was so reassuring, with his precise diction and his courteous manner. She thought that she should not have gone to Colin's dentist. She would go back to Mr Macgregor, she decided, because one should stick to a good dentist: loyalty meant something in those relationships. She glanced at the trench again. She remembered what he had said. She turned away.

She knew the McAdam pet shop; she had often driven past it on her way to Julie's Designs. It was just on a busy road and had a large sign outside: *All Things for All Our Furred and Feathered Friends: Proprietor, Henry McAdam*. She had never had occasion to enter the shop, but she had found herself wondering about Henry McAdam. What sort of man would he be? She thought of him as a sort of contemporary Dr Dolittle, able to divine the needs of animals, tirelessly providing all the bits and pieces that ownership of even an undemanding and very ordinary pet seemed to require. Now, as she stood before its front display window, she could make out Henry McAdam behind the counter inside, engaged in conversation with a customer.

As she went inside, her opening of the door triggered

an old-fashioned mechanical bell. Henry McAdam looked up from what he was doing and gave her a welcoming smile. "Just a moment," he said.

He finished serving the other customer, who thanked him and went off with her parcel of goods. Henry McAdam rang something up on a till before approaching Rose. Her attention had been attracted by a display cage, in which a family of guinea pigs huddled together in a bed of curling paper shavings.

"Lovely little things, aren't they?" Henry said.

"Yes," said Rose. "Although I never quite know where they fit in. They're not mice or rats, are they? Are they something to do with squirrels?"

"*Caviidae*," said Henry. "Rodents, actually. That's all one needs to bear in mind. These ones were not in very good shape when I got them. They had been kept in a cage with a floor of sawdust. Sawdust produces tiny splinters that irritate their skin, poor things. Well-meaning, but not a good idea. They're much more comfortable now, with paper, as you can see.

Rose shook her head. "I wouldn't have known."

"Are you interested?"

Rose laughed. "No, I wasn't thinking of guinea pigs."

Henry looked expectant.

"Dog treats," said Rose. "I was looking for something that a dog would find irresistible. A treat that no dog can refuse."

Henry stroked his chin. "Big dog or small dog?"

"Big," said Rose. "Massive. A Rottweiler-cross."

Henry's expression was one of distaste. "I imagine

that he eats you out of house and home. Those large, thick-set dogs have an awful appetite."

"He's not mine," said Rose quickly. "He belongs to a friend of mine."

"Ah," said Henry. "A present. Well, that's very thoughtful of you. And I think I have just the ticket for you."

He went behind the counter and extracted a packet from a shelf on the wall. "These are called Dogs' Delights," he said. "I don't know what they put in them, but dogs go wild over them. It's the canine equivalent of catnip, I suppose."

"That sounds ideal," said Rose.

"People keep saying that the manufacturers of some of these pet foods put nicotine into them. The idea is that they make the cat or dog into an addict."

Rose looked disapproving. "Nicotine?"

"I think it's one of those urban legends," said Henry, passing her the large packet of Dogs' Delights. "They list the contents, and I see no mention of anything untoward. If animals appear to be addicted, it's probably just because they like the taste."

"And dogs really go for these?" Rose asked.

"Yes," said Henry. "They love them. They're large, boned-shaped biscuits. They're very meaty, which explains the price. They aren't cheap. But as an occasional treat, they're very good value."

"They sound just what I want," said Rose.

"Good."

Henry put the treats into a paper bag. Rose gave him

her credit card, and he completed the transaction.

"Would you like to go on our mailing list?" he asked.

She almost said yes, out of politeness, but stopped herself in time. She realised that she would rather that nobody knew about this transaction, and so she did not want to leave any further evidence of her having been there. Already, by proffering the credit card, she had left an electronic footprint.

"I don't think there's much point," she said. "This is just a one-off present. Thank you anyway."

She left the shop and returned to her car. She noticed that her heart seemed to be beating faster than usual. I have done nothing wrong, she said to herself. I have done nothing wrong *yet*, that is.

That evening, Colin was home later than usual, having been obliged, rather against his will, to attend an early evening drinks party organised by a client. He attended such corporate occasions faithfully, but he did not like them. "Small talk depresses me," he said. "And these functions rarely rise above that. Golf, holidays – that sort of chatter gets me down. I feel I want to suddenly shout out something shocking and bring the whole thing down about my ears. But, of course, I never will – don't worry."

"I know you'd never do anything stupid," Rose said. "You're far too intelligent."

"Far too feart," said Colin, using the Scots word for "afraid".

She thought, And me? Will I ever do anything stupid?

People who did stupid things – really unwise things – were usually those who were bad at joined-up thinking. They did not link cause and effect. They did not think things through sufficiently to see what would happen. I am not like that, she thought. I will take a risk, where a risk needs to be taken, but I'll be fully aware of what might happen. I'll decide what to do on the basis of what the odds are of any particular result. If you did that, then your actions would be calculated, rather than chaotic, as some people's behaviour was. It was simple common sense, really: don't do anything you may regret. Why anybody should find it hard to follow that rule escaped her.

Because Colin was late home after his drinks party, they did not sit down to dinner until almost nine. Colin liked something simple when he had been out earlier in the evening, and so Rose served the twice-cooked goat cheese soufflé that she knew was one of his favourites. With this, they had a walnut salad and roasted red Romano peppers. Rose poured them each a glass of white wine, which Colin sampled and described as "pleasantly flinty".

He looked at her. "I'm very fortunate," he said.

She watched him across the table. Of course he was fortunate – just look at him.

But that was not what he meant. "You know, I sometimes think of what my life would have been like if we hadn't met one another at Vicky's party. I think about that, and you know something? It can make me break out in a cold sweat, because so much of our life is just chance, isn't it? We may meet the right person at the right time, or we may just miss that person by a hair's breadth – by this much." He held up a thumb and forefinger, separated by the tiniest space. "Yes, by that much. It could happen – in fact, it probably happens all the time."

"Maybe," she said.

"And then we tell ourselves that we were somehow meant to meet the other person – the person we marry, for instance. We convince ourselves that it was all destined to be, that the planets were all lined up just so that we could meet one another, but it doesn't work that way, of course. Our human affairs are nothing when looked at against the background of the planets shooting around in space. Nothing. *We're* nothing. We like to think we're everything, but, in reality, we're nothing."

Rose nodded. Colin was being unusually talkative, which must be the effect of the wine, she thought. He must have had something to drink at the business party earlier in the evening, and now there was the pleasantly flinty wine to further loosen his tongue.

"I said I was fortunate," Colin continued. "What I meant was that I am lucky to have you."

Rose blushed. She did not mind being complimented, but she was surprised by Colin's unaccustomed loquacity. She replied, "I'm the fortunate one. I'm lucky to have you."

He shook his head. "No, it's me – I don't know what I would have done if I hadn't met you."

She made light of this. "You would have found somebody else. I don't think you would have struggled."

"I'm not so sure," he said. He yawned. "I'm really tired."

"I'm not surprised," she said. "A trying day at work, and then being on duty at the party. You must be shattered."

"I'm going to go to bed," he said. "I know it's early . . ."

"I'll stay up a bit," said Rose. "There are one or two things I have to do." One thing in particular, she thought.

They finished the goat cheese soufflé and, although Colin offered to clear up, Rose insisted he go to bed. She loaded the dishwasher and tidied the kitchen. She turned out the downstairs lights but did not go upstairs. Rather, she left the house by a side door and made her way to one of the garages. She had left it unlocked and went inside, closing the door behind her, before she turned on the light. The cardboard box was waiting for her, ready to be cut for its new purpose. It had contained the new fridge that had been delivered the previous week, and she had been intending to cut it into small enough pieces to allow it to be put in the recycling bin. Fortunately, she had not got round to that and was now able to cut the box into wide strips, four or five feet in length. She made six of these, and then, stacking them together, she switched off the garage light and made her way out into the garden.

The cardboard strips were exactly right for the purpose she had envisaged for them. Laid out side by side across the top of the trench in the garden, they completely concealed the void beneath them. A few handfuls of soil scattered across the top served as camouflage, so the fact that there was a deep trench below the cardboard was not readily apparent, especially at night.

She went back into the kitchen, making sure once more not to turn on any lights. She had left the dog treats on the table, and now she took these, opening the bag as she went back into the garden. She sniffed at the air; even the human nose could detect the strong meaty aroma that arose from the bone-shaped biscuits. Henry McAdam had been right: any dog would go wild over a smell like that. She smiled at the prospect that lay ahead. There was no real victory in outwitting a dog, but there was a distinct pleasure in teaching one a much-needed lesson. What she was doing was not cruel: it was simply an obedience lesson, a necessary intervention to bring an ill-behaved dog into line. That was in the dog's interest, surely, every bit as much as it might be in the interests of suffering neighbours.

The moon had gone behind a cloud, but there was still enough light for Rose to make her way safely to the edge of the trench. Bending forward – but being careful not to put any weight on the layer of cardboard she had put in place – Rose tossed a handful of Dogs' Delights into the middle of the trap. Then, just to be on the safe side, she added a few more, scattered closer to the edge this time. If Monty found these, he would then be tempted to go further to wolf down the others. And as he did that, the cardboard would give way under his weight and collapse into the depths of the trench, along with its canine burden. That would teach him. The trench was far too deep for him to be able to climb out of it, and he would spend an uncomfortable night down below, reflecting – if dogs could ever reflect – on the consequences of straying out of his own territory. He would learn a lesson, Rose hoped, but more than that, she would have the satisfaction of paying him back for what he had done. He had destroyed her garlic bed. She had been so excited by the thought of a garlic crop, and he had wrecked it. She hated him for it. She wanted to punish him – and his owner too – and she would do just that. She was not normally vindictive, but this was different; this was special.

She went back into the house, closing the door behind her after hesitating, just for a moment, on the doorstep. Should I really be doing this? she thought. Was it not perhaps even a bit cruel to lure a dog, even an ill-tempered dog like Monty, into a trap? It was not as if she was planning to hurt him – a dog of that size would hardly be damaged by tumbling into an earth pit – but, even so, it might be just a little bit harsh. But then she thought of how else she might make her point to both Monty and Tiger, and she decided that there was no other obvious way. There was no point in trying to talk to Tiger; she must have been only too aware of her neighbour's annoyance. No, she would proceed with her plan – it was just too delicious to abandon. It was very sweet revenge, indeed. It was compensation for the garlic that was never to be. It was about garlic, and yearning, and disappointment, and justice. It was about so many different things.

Colin was asleep when she went into their bedroom. She looked at his head on the pillow and wondered what he dreamed about. He said that he did not remember his dreams, and that he doubted whether he dreamed at all. She told him that everybody dreamed and, if he did not remember what he dreamed about, it was simply because he had never trained himself to commit the dreams to memory. He listened but was unconvinced. "I still think I don't dream," he insisted.

She undressed and slipped into her nightie. She had a magazine on her bedside table and paged through it, but she found that she could not concentrate. She was thinking of Tiger. What was it like to be Tiger, she wondered. What was it like to have hair like that, piled up on top of your head? Was it uncomfortable? Did the beehive move in high winds? Would rain flatten it?

And what was it like to live with somebody like Ray, with his muscles and tattooed arms? What could you talk about with a man like that? If, in fact, he was a man like that – for Rose suddenly realised that she had never actually met him, and she was judging him purely on a fleeting glimpse of him getting out of their car and then driving off to Aberdeen. Yet a mere glimpse could tell a whole story, and she felt that there would be no surprises in store if she ever were to get to know him better. That is not to say I don't have an open mind, she thought. I am *not* my mother . . . yet.

She drifted off to sleep, thinking of Tiger and Ray and

Mr Macgregor's wife with her poodles, and of the garlic strewn all over the wrecked bed in the vegetable garden. Just after two, she was woken by a noise from outside. She had been in a light sleep, and she was instantly awake. It was not a bark; it was more of a yelp. And then there came another sound – a thud of some sort.

She smiled in the darkness. That was Monty falling for the bait. That was the wretched dog being taught a long overdue lesson. She strained to hear what she thought would follow – the desperate barking that might waken Tiger and bring her out to investigate her dog's misfortune. But there was nothing, and Rose wondered whether she had imagined it. She considered getting up to see if anything had happened, but she decided not to go outside. She would not like to meet Tiger – or Monty, for that matter – in the dark.

She managed to get back to sleep and did not wake up again until Colin brought her a cup of tea at seven the following morning. He was going off to work early, he said, and would skip breakfast. "Take care," he said.

"Of course," she said. And then she asked, "Have you heard any barking from our canine friend?"

He shook his head. Every morning when Monty was let out of the house at about six thirty, he would spend several minutes barking. That had not happened.

"He must be sleeping in." Colin said. "I suppose dogs do that from time to time."

Rose did not reply, but she was wide awake now.

She blew Colin a kiss as he left the room and then drank her cup of tea, rather too quickly, slightly scalding her mouth. She heard him leave the house as she got out of bed and began to dress. The day outside, she noticed, was a fine one: the air still and the sky clear of cloud. She would have a leisurely breakfast and then go to Julie's Designs, although her presence there was not really necessary at the moment, such was the competence and enthusiasm of her assistant. If she wanted to spend a few hours in the garden before going into town, that would be perfectly all right. A few hours in the garden . . . She had put the matter out of her mind, deliberately, but now it came back to her. Monty.

She went out into the garden. Walking round the side of the house, she was able to see the trench and the piles of earth beside it. She stopped, straining her ears for some sound. None came. She took a few steps, nonchalantly, as if undecided what to do. She need not have bothered – from that part of the garden she could not be observed from the neighbours on either side. She approached the trench and saw that the cardboard covering had either been removed or fallen into the trap. Her heart gave a leap.

She decided to call Monty's name, and she did so now, softly at first, and then slightly louder. She stopped to listen. There was no response. She knew what she had to do, of course: she would have to approach the trench and peer down into it to see if the dog was still there. She took a step forward and stopped again. She was unable to face it. Monty must be there, but he must be dead. She had killed him. He had fallen into the trap and broken his neck. That explained the silence.

The awful realisation dawned: I have killed my neighbour's dog.

She took a deep breath. This was ridiculous; she should go and look into the trench. The cardboard might have simply given way. There might have been rain, for all she knew, and cardboard loses its stiffness if it gets wet. She took a step forward, but she could not bring herself to go on. She could not face looking down at the corpse of her victim.

She called Monty once more, again with no response. Then, reaching down, she picked up a handful of small stones and tossed these into the mouth of the trench, still refusing to look. She heard the stones fall to the bottom of the trench. Nothing happened.

Now irrational fear took over. Running back towards the garage, in which she kept her gardening tools, Rose fetched a shovel. Returning to the nearest pile of earth, she began to push the soil into the trench, still not daring to look at what she was covering up. She worked furiously, ignoring the sweat that now began to make large damp patches on her blouse. For half an hour she worked without a break, making a significant impact on the piles of earth beside the trench. Then she stood back and, after a brief moment of hesitation, forced herself to look over the side of the trench. She was surprised to see that she had nearly filled it, and got back to work quickly, completing the task shortly afterwards. By the time an hour was up, there was no more earth to be shovelled and, dropping her shovel where she stood, she began to make her way back to the house. But as she did so, something caught her eye: a bright glint of metal in the grass close to the now filled-in trench. Reaching down, she picked the object up: a small key ring with two keys attached and a silver letter "T", executed in a childish, florid style. She frowned. Was this something dropped by one of the council workmen when they had first come to dig the trench? Surely not. No workman digging a trench would carry something like this.

And then the realisation dawned on her. These were Tiger's keys; they had to be. The initial raised the supposition, and the aesthetics of the "T" provided the confirmation. But what had Tiger been doing in her garden? She froze. Tiger had heard Monty fall into the trench, or she had been woken by his howling for help. Rose herself must have slept through that, but Tiger had heard. And then she had tried to rescue her dog and, in the process, had fallen in. She had broken her neck – it was perfectly possible to do that if you fell in a trench.

And then she had lain there – already dead, perhaps – next to Monty, until the perpetrator of all this had come out and started shovelling soil over them. The thought halted Rose in her tracks, and for a moment she stood quite still as a wave of terror passed over her. She had killed somebody. It was her fault. It was a moment of unfathomable horror, unmitigated in any way. She tried to say to herself, "This is an accident," but it came out as, "This is no accident." She had dug the trap deliberately, hoping that Monty would fall into it. Had she thought for a moment, it should have occurred to her that not only might a dog fall into it, but a person. Of course, she should have thought of that, but she had not, and now that precise disaster had happened.

She felt weak. She wanted to think. She made her way into the house and sat down, not on a chair, but on the floor. She struggled to breathe. She closed her eyes, as if that might eradicate or conceal what had happened, but when she opened them, the world was still there – that world in which she had done this terrible, irreversible thing.

She felt something sharp in her hand and realised that she was still grasping the keys she had picked up. And there came to her the first glimmer of hope. All of this was surmise. She had not seen Monty, and she had not seen Tiger. If only she had looked into the trench, she might have seen that it was empty. Of course, it was empty; of course, it was . . . She now tried to persuade herself that none of this had actually taken place. What really happened was this: Tiger had come outside in the night in response to Monty's howling. In the course of her rescue of the dog – requiring only the sort of ladder that everyone had in their house – she had dropped her keys. That was all. And even while Rose sat there, abject on the floor, Tiger was no doubt enjoying a leisurely cup of coffee in her own kitchen while she watched one of those inane daytime television shows that she must surely like to watch, with Monty, unharmed, sleeping at her feet, already having forgotten – as dogs must do – the unfortunate experiences of the night.

She immediately brightened and picked herself up from the floor. It was now clear what she had to do. She would put out of her mind these ridiculous fantasies and go over to Tiger's house. She would ring the bell and give Tiger the keys, telling her that she had found them in her garden and, by implication, censuring her for trespassing there. It was Tiger who should be feeling guilty, because Monty had no business coming into *her* garden and falling into *her* trench.

She left the house and made her way to Tiger's front door, passing the trench on the way but not afraid now to look at it. This was not a grave, after all, not the scene of any crime; it was a perfectly ordinary patch of dug-over ground; it was no more than that.

She reached Tiger's front door. It was slightly ajar.

She took a deep breath. People left their door open for all sorts of reasons. The weather was warm; there had been a high-pressure zone hanging over the country, slow to shift. Of course one might leave one's front door open, to encourage a through-breeze.

She pushed the button of the doorbell and heard it ring within the house. Westminster Chimes, she noted – how typical, she thought; how suburban; how *frilly*. Why not have a simple ring – as she and Colin did? It went with the beehive hairstyle and the key ring with its fancy initial, and having a husband who had tattooed arms, and a dog like Monty, and . . . everything, really.

She waited a few seconds before ringing once more. Again, there was no answer. Now she felt alarm creep up on her again. She pushed the door open gingerly, as a burglar might test a breach of security. The door opened into an entrance hall. There was a table against the wall on one side and pegs on which coats were hung. An umbrella with a plastic canopy lay on the ground, as if dropped there. On the table there was a mobile phone and a yellow plastic ball-point pen.

"Anybody home?" Rose called out, trying to sound confident, but her voice cracking under the strain of the moment.

The house was silent. She called again, stepping into the hall now, and then a third time. There was no response. She swallowed hard. A door off the hall led into the kitchen – she could see the fridge from where she was standing – and she went through that into a large, well-equipped kitchen, gleaming with glass surfaces and shining appliances. She stopped. In the centre of the room was a table with two chairs. On the table was a tea-pot, a cup, and a plate. The plate had a half-eaten piece of toast on it – she could see the teeth-marks where Tiger had taken a bite. The cup was half full of tea.

She stepped back in horror. Her initial fears must be right. This was a house that had been walked out of by somebody who did not come back in. What she had imagined to have happened must have taken place. She had killed Monty. She had killed Tiger.

Rose stumbled her way through the rest of the house, just to be sure. She searched everywhere, except for one room, which was locked. She knocked on the door, but of course there was no reply, and she turned away.

She returned to the hall and went outside, closing the door behind her. She reached for the key ring in her pocket and inserted one of the keys in the lock. It fitted perfectly, just as she imagined it would. Making sure that the door was locked, she then posted the key ring and keys back through the letterbox.

She began to walk back down the garden path. As she did so, she saw somebody coming towards her. She stopped, her heart thumping loudly, her breathing short. She saw that it was the postman, Graham.

She said the first thing that came into her mind. "No reply. She's not in, Graham."

He greeted her and then said, "Doesn't matter. No parcels – just some letters that will fit in the slot. Nothing large."

He was looking at her, smiling. Was there something unusual about his expression? Had he seen her coming out of the house? If he had, then he might be wondering why she should have said that there was no reply. She remembered something her mother had said to her when she young: *Once you start to deceive, there's no stopping.* Deceit built upon deceit until the whole edifice of lies came tumbling down.

The postman carried on to Tiger's front door while Rose returned to her house. Once inside, she stood still for a moment, clasping and unclasping her hands in an agony of regret. The thought that gnaws at the conscience of so many wrongdoers now occupied hers: If only I could turn the clock back to the moment before I did what I did; if only I could do that.

She went into the kitchen and called Colin. He was in a meeting and sounded distracted. "It's not a very convenient time," he told her before she managed to say anything.

She struggled to speak.

"Are you all right?" asked Colin, his tone now one of concern.

"Yes," she said. "I am. But no, not really."

"What's wrong?"

"Something has happened."

Now Colin's anxiety was obvious. "Something? What something?"

"Monty—" she began.

He cut her short. "Has he been in the garden again? Have you spoken to her? To Tiger?"

"Colin," she said, "please come home. I know you're busy at work, but I need you. Right now. Please."

He hesitated for a moment before replying. He would be home within half an hour. In the meantime, she was to sit down and wait for him. "Make yourself tea," he said. "And don't do anything else. Nothing. Do you understand?"

He rang off, and she sat down, hunched in misery, close to tears, but too shocked, perhaps, to do something as simple and as human as burst out crying. She told herself that she had not meant to harm Monty – that she had only wanted to discourage him. It was not her fault that he must have fallen in an awkward position and suffered serious damage. And it was certainly not her fault that Tiger had come out and fallen into the trench herself. What could she expect if she went out under cover of darkness and began to prowl around her neighbour's garden? She had only herself to blame for that.

But none of that provided more than the briefest moment of respite. The awful truth was that she, Rose, had set the whole thing in motion. She had wound up the clockwork mechanism of events and started it on the course that led ineluctably to this result. She was the cause of what had happened; it was her responsibility alone, and if the truth were ever to come out, then she would serve – quite deservedly – a long prison sentence for . . . What did they call it? Culpable homicide – that was the term. She would be convicted of culpable homicide, if not murder. It would be in the newspapers. Her friends would be appalled. She imagined their reaction, as reported in the press: *We never suspected she was capable of killing somebody – not once . . .* Nobody suspects that of their friends, of course, and then the friends turn out to be capable of the most terrible things, as almost all of us are, if conditions are right; we all have Cain within us, not far from the surface, ready to nudge us into atavism.

Colin sat opposite her at the kitchen table.

"Take a deep breath," he said. "Just take a breath."

She clenched her teeth. "I am breathing. I never stopped."

He sighed. "It's no use your snapping at me. All I'm suggesting you do is calm down. That's all." He paused.

He saw that she was now doing as he suggested and taking a deep breath. That should help, he thought.

"Tell me what happened," he said, trying to sound reassuring but not succeeding entirely. "Things are often not so bad when you spell them out."

But they were; and when she had finished telling him about what happened, his eyes were wide with concern. "You didn't look in the trench?" he asked. "Not at all?"

She shook her head. "Not until it was half filled up."

Colin closed his eyes. Now he took a deep breath. "All right," he said, opening his eyes again. "Let's not panic. I must admit I am a bit put out by what you've told me, but . . ." He raised a finger. "But let's just look at it in a cool and rational manner. Was there any evidence that anybody – dog or human – was in the trench?" He did not wait for her to reply; instead answering his own question. "There was nothing. Not a single bit of evidence."

"And the key?" Rose asked. "What about the key?"

"That could have been dropped at any time. And it's possible that Tiger went out to rescue Monty. She might have dropped it then."

"And then gone back to the house?" asked Rose.

"Precisely."

Rose thought for a moment. "Why was her door open?'

Colin shrugged. "She might have gone out and forgotten to close it. People do that, you know."

Rose was not convinced. "I don't think so," she said.

In attempting to convince his wife that she had

nothing to worry about, Colin had succeeded in convincing himself. "There'll be a perfectly innocent explanation," he said. "You have no need to worry. None at all." He paused. "Things like . . . like what you think happened, just don't happen here. Not in Balerno. Nor in Edinburgh, for that matter. They just don't."

Rose stared at him. "Then where do they happen?"

"In fiction," Colin said. "In films. Not in real life. And definitely not in the real life that happens around here."

Rose transferred her gaze to the floor. The she looked up. "Could we go over and check?"

Colin stood up. "Good idea," he said. 'We'll go and take a look-round. She may even have come back by now."

"From where?"

"I don't know," said Colin, a bit impatiently. "Really, Rose, this is a big fuss over nothing."

Over murder, she thought.

They went out into the garden, skirting the trench – the scene of the crime, Rose thought – and into Tiger's garden. Colin went up to the front door and pressed the bell, turning to grin at Rose as he did so. He waited a few moments and then rang again. From within the house, they heard a telephone ringing in the hall. Leaning forward to press his ear against the letterbox, Colin listened as the answering machine picking up the call.

"You have reached Tiger and Ray," Tiger's recorded

voice announced. "I cannot get to the phone right now . . ."

Or ever again, thought Rose.

". . . so please leave a message after the tone."

It was all very clear, as was the voice that spoke after the tone.

"Tiger? This is Marge. Look, where are you, for heaven's sake? You said we'd meet at the tennis club at eight. I was there, on the dot. Why the no-show? Give me a call and we can book the court for some other time. Don't worry, I'll let you win – as usual."

The voice cut off and the machine became silent. Rose turned and looked at Colin, who had heard the message too. He seemed less confident now.

"See?" said Rose, adding, "You heard that. See?"

Colin stepped back. "Did you try the back door?"

Rose shook her head.

"Then let's."

They went round to the back door. It was locked, and there was no sign of life when they looked through the kitchen window and then through the windows on either side of the house. When they went round to the front once more, Colin said, "Well, I suppose the next thing to do is excavate the trench."

Rose grabbed his arm. "No, Colin," she said. "We can't."

Colin sighed. "Well, how else are we going to establish that what you are worrying about is highly unlikely –" here, he repeated himself to drive home the point – "highly unlikely to have occurred. How else?"

"I can't face it," said Rose. "I just can't. And anyway, what if people saw us digging? You can see the trench from the road. What if somebody saw us?"

"But people often dig in their gardens," Colin pointed out. "It's an entirely innocent activity."

But Rose shook her head. "I want to get away, Colin," she said. "I just want to get away for a few days. I can't face being here right now."

Colin frowned. "You can't run away from things, you know," he said.

Her nerves were frayed, and she snapped back at him, "I'm not running away from anything. I just want to get away for a few days. Can't you just drop everything for forty-eight hours? You're a partner, after all – the firm can't tell you what to do."

"Oh, really, Rose . . ."

She began to sob. "I can't bear it, Colin. I can't bear being here with that –" she gestured towards the trench – "with that reminder."

He moved to put his arm around her. "Darling, you mustn't let this silly thing upset you so. Let me dig, show you that there's nothing there, and then we can put the whole thing to rest."

She pushed him away. Now she screamed, her voice rising in a shrill crescendo, "No, no, no! You mustn't do that. You mustn't dig." She became pleading. "Please, darling. I beg you. Please don't."

He held her against him. He felt her tears on the back of his hand. He leaned forward and kissed her brows. "Silly darling," he whispered. "If you really want to, we'll go up north for a couple of days. Crieff Hydro? I'll see if they have a room."

Crieff Hydro was a large Highland hotel, built in the Scots Jacobean style, surrounded by the hills of Perthshire. Its history as a hydropathic institution gave it a sedate, rather old-fashioned atmosphere that still appealed not only to families but also to those who appreciated walks in the forests, healthy bouts of swimming, and gentle rounds of golf.

"I love this place," said Colin, as they came to a halt in the hotel car park. "I used to come here as a boy, you know. I had my fist kiss over there." He pointed to a cluster of rhododendrons.

Rose glanced in the direction that he was pointing. She said nothing.

He turned to her. "Are you all right?"

She nodded mutely. How does it feel to have killed somebody, she asked herself. And then thought, It feels like this – just like this.

Colin looked concerned but tried to jolly her on. "Let's go and check in," he said. "Then we can go for a walk before dinner. I'm building up an appetite."

They were shown to their room, which overlooked a lawn on which a small group of people were playing croquet. They heard their laughter drift up from below. In the distance, the hills were an attenuated blue.

"This is such a beautiful country," said Colin, as he gazed out of the window. "Look at those blue hills. They're like watercolours."

She glanced; then she turned away.

"My darling," he said. "I can see that you're suffering. You mustn't, you know. You've done nothing wrong."

She stared at him. *Nothing wrong?* Did he even begin to understand what she had done? Did he have the slightest inkling of how she felt – under this great cloud of guilt and remorse? It was not his fault. Nobody could understand the anguish of accidental slayers, other than accidental slayers themselves.

They went out for a walk. Following a path that led into the trees, they found themselves gaining ground, looking down at the towers of the Hydro from above. The croquet players on the lawn were small black dots now; a dog ran across the grass, pursued by two children, the size of ants.

Suddenly, she stopped and grasped Colin's arm. Not far away, on a path that led in a different direction, she had spotted another couple. They were disappearing into the trees, and she did not get a good view of them, but the woman had a beehive hairstyle – she was sure of that.

"What is it?" asked Colin.

"Th-there," stuttered Rose. "Those people."

The other couple were just a flash of colour in the forest; now they were gone.

"What about them?"

Rose's voice was tiny. "I'm sure I saw Tiger."

He looked at her. "Where?"

She waved a hand. "Those people. The woman. That was Tiger."

He looked over his shoulder in the direction that she had pointed. "I can't see anybody."

"That's because they've gone.'

He turned to look at her again, more searchingly now. "You saw somebody?"

She nodded. "A couple. A man and a woman. The woman was Tiger – or looked pretty much like her."

He sighed. "Looked like her . . . Lots of people look like other people, Rose. That man in the reception down there – at the Hydro – you know who he looked like? Andy Murray – the tennis player."

"Maybe it was."

"What would Andy Murray be doing working in the Crieff Hydro?"

She shrugged.

He tried to be patient. "All I'm saying is this: you're imagining things. You've had a shock. The human mind is . . ." He was not sure what he wanted to say. The human mind is susceptible? The human mind is suggestible?

"It was her," muttered Rose.

He looked again into the trees, to where the other path disappeared. "I don't think it can have been her," he said quietly.

"Because she's in that trench?"

He kept a level tone. "I didn't say that. You know I didn't say that."

He took her arm and led her back down the track towards the hotel. They returned to their room, where Colin ran a deep bath in the old-fashioned tub. "I feel like soaking," he said.

She lay down on the bed and closed her eyes. She saw the trench. She saw council workmen coming back and scratching their heads. Then, in her mind, they picked up their shovels and began to dig out the earth. She wanted to stop them, but they paid no attention to her, and very quickly the trench was empty again. She looked into it. Tiger was sitting on a small pile of soil. She looked up at Rose and smiled at her. Monty, at her feet, opened an eye, and then closed it again, as tired dogs may do, not wanting to raise themselves from their slumbers.

"There you are," said Tiger, and added, "I've been waiting for you."

Rose opened her eyes again. She wondered whether this was what madness was like. Perhaps it came upon you in exactly this way, leading you into increasingly troubled fantasies. And then, finally, unable to escape the torment, you lapsed into incoherence.

Colin had his bath. Then, when he had changed into fresh clothes – Rose did not bother to change – they went down to dinner.

A waitress came out of the swing doors that led into the kitchen. She stopped and looked in Rose's direction. Rose met her gaze and gave a little gasp.

"What is it?" asked Colin.

"That waitress . . ."

Colin glanced towards the waitress, who was making her way towards a table on the other side of the dining room. "What about her?"

"I know you'll be cross with me."

Colin frowned. "I won't. Of course I won't be cross with you."

"It's Tiger. I could swear it's Tiger."

Colin did not bother to look. He reached out across the table and took Rose's hand. "Darling, I don't think you're well."

"It's her," whispered Rose. "I'm sure it's her."

Colin sat back in his seat. "That's it," he said. "We're going home tomorrow morning. And I am going to excavate that trench and show you there's nothing there."

She opened her mouth to say something, but no words came.

"Understand?" said Colin. "That's what I'm going to do. This has gone far enough."

She found her voice, at last. "And then what? Are you going to turn me in to the police?"

"Oh, don't be so ridiculous. This is all in your imagination. There's nothing to hand you in over. Nothing at all." He paused. "We'll go home first thing tomorrow. I'm sorry, but that's what I want to do. Full stop."

Rose found it difficult to get to sleep that night. Eventually she drifted off, but her night was fitful and disturbed. In the morning, she did not go down for breakfast with Colin, saying that she was not hungry. He had a quick meal and then came back to pick her up from the room. Once in the car, they set off in silence and did not speak until they reached the bridge over the Forth; she said something about the rail bridge in the distance, and he simply nodded and made a non-committal remark.

Once at the house, he helped her in with her case and then went off to fetch a shovel.

"I wish you wouldn't," she said.

"I have to," he answered. "We can't go on like this." He looked at her imploringly. "Are you going to come with me?"

She shook her head. "Oh, my God," she muttered. "I can't believe this is happening."

"Well, if you change your mind . . ." He went outside. He did not care who saw him. You were entitled to dig in your own garden if you so desired. He dug.

It was hot, uncomfortable work. The air was dank in the trench, and the earth got in his hair, his nose, his eyes. But he continued, tossing each spadeful up into the sky, not caring whether some of it rained down on him. He half believed that he would find nothing at the bottom of the trench – just a water main – but he also half believed that at any moment his shovel would dig into something soft – a leg, or the flank of a dog – and if that happened, he had no idea what he would do. He rehearsed possibilities: he could make a clean breast of things with the police. They would see that it was all an accident, and that Rose was innocent of any serious crime. But then again, they might not: they might disbelieve everything he said – they may even think that he was the one who had killed Tiger. Of course, it was always open to him to fill in the trench again. Then they could put the house on the market and get away altogether. They could go to live in Glasgow – it had been said to him often that there was a seat waiting for him in the company's branch over there. If they did that, then Tiger's disappearance would remain a mystery for all time. It would be no more than another unsolved cold case. That sort of thing was not uncommon, and eventually everybody forgot about them.

He heard a voice above him, and for a moment he thought that Rose had relented and come out to see how he was getting on.

"You look busy."

It was Tiger.

Colin dropped his shovel. He took a step backwards, bumping against the side of the trench. Small pebbles fell like rain.

"Sorry to give you a fright," Tiger said. "I just thought I'd check that everything was all right. I wasn't sure who might be digging up your garden."

There was a sudden bark, and Monty appeared beside his mistress. He looked down into the trench, a long line of saliva dribbling down from his fleshy jaws. The pungent-smelling saliva touched Colin's face. He retched.

"Careful, Monty," said Tiger. "You wouldn't want to fall into that." She looked sharply at Colin. "You wouldn't want him to do that, would you?"

Tiger looked at her watch. "I must dash, Colin," she said. "Ray is coming back from Aberdeen any moment. I must get his lunch ready. Good luck with . . . with whatever it is that you're doing."

Over lunch, Tiger told Ray what had happened. "Poor Monty fell into a trap that horrid woman had dug," she said. "I went out to rescue him. It was pitch dark. Horrible."

Ray picked a piece of ham out of his teeth. "Poor Tiger," he said. "Poor sweetie-pie."

"I know," said Tiger. "I almost fell in myself."

"Tut-tut," said Ray. "We're always very careful on the rigs."

"But I didn't," Tiger went on. "Then the next morning I saw her come out to see whether she'd caught poor Monty. I watched her with your binoculars. She was obviously dead worried. She wouldn't look into the trench, and I realised that she thought some dreadful thing had happened."

Ray frowned. "I'm not sure—"

Tiger interrupted him. "She came over here to look for us, so I hid in the spare bedroom with Monty. She searched the house and obviously thought I was in the trench she had just filled in. I could just imagine how she felt."

Ray now looked uncomfortable. He shifted in his seat. He took another piece of ham. "And then?" he said.

"I let her stew," said Tiger. "They went off somewhere, and I imagine that she had a sleepless night. Serves her right."

Ray put down his fork. "You shouldn't have done that," he said. "That was cruel."

"I was just getting even," Tiger protested. "She asked for it."

Ray stared at her, his eyes narrowed. He felt tired. It was hard – far too hard, and he had no further energy for the deception that it involved. "I may as well tell you," he said. "I've met somebody up in Aberdeen. I'm having an affair."

Tiger was silent. "You wouldn't," she whispered. Then she went on, "Tell me, Ray – tell me – you wouldn't, would you?"

"I would," he said. "And I'll tell you something else, Tiger – she would never do something like this. Never."

Tiger and Ray separated three weeks later. She went off, with Monty, to spend a few months with a friend from school who had a house in the Borders. The friend introduced her to a local dairy farmer, Brian, who admired her greatly. "Never change your hairstyle," he said earnestly. "Never." They married eight months later, after the divorce came through. Monty loved the Borders. He also loved Brian, who had a nice smell, from a dog's point of view.

Ray apologised to Rose and, separately and more freely, to Colin. "I'm ashamed of what Tiger did," he said.

"And I'm ashamed of what I did," said Rose. "But thank you so much for saying that you are ashamed."

"It's what you have to do," said Ray. "You have to say sorry."

He and Colin became good friends. They went bowling together with two other friends of Ray's – Eddie and Gordon. Sometimes they went to the pub after bowling. Gordon told them how he used to be a ballet dancer. Colin was not sure whether to believe him, and his incredulity showed. "I'm not making this up," said Gordon. "I was. I swear I was."

"He was," said Ray.

DIGNITY

&

DECENCY

An Introduction

Our celebrity culture encourages all the wrong values. It creates a world of inflated egos, in which people behave with discourtesy to others and with scant regard to that old-fashioned virtue: modesty. That is one of the issues that occurs in this next story, set in the literary world – the world of editors and book festivals. There are two heroes here: one is a young man who carries with him the burden of unrequited love. For some, that is a sentence under which they serve their life. He does so with dignity and decency, as many do. Then there is a Mr A.J. Canavan, an Irishman, whom we never meet, but about whose virtues we hear. The good that people do may be felt well after they have left us – and it may be felt in ways that we do not anticipate.

A central issue about revenge is addressed in this story, and sides are taken. Revenge may be entertaining, but ultimately, we must acknowledge that to exact revenge is the wrong thing to do. It just is. Mercy and forgiveness are important goods that we must stress at every opportunity. We have to forgive, rather than seek revenge. Remember Nelson Mandela, that gracious and good man, who embodied that so demonstrably. Forgiveness heals; it allows us to unclutter our lives with the business of the past; it makes room for human flourishing. It also facilitates the happy ending, which is what we want in most, if not all, the books we read, and in life too.

ONE, TWO, THREE

One

"A degree in English literature? Me?"

Yes, thought Sam. That is exactly what I want. Exactly. And it had been his ambition, right from his teenage years, when an inspirational English teacher interested him in the novels of Anthony Trollope and Charles Dickens. His favourite was *The Pickwick Papers*, which he read three times by the age of sixteen. But he also enjoyed *Barchester Towers*, because he thought Slope was such a vivid, detestable character – as was the bishop's wife. Hateful people, both of them. Slightly later, he went through a D.H. Lawrence phase, followed by a spell of reading Jack Kerouac. He also read the Fitzgerald translation of *The Odyssey*, and the poets of the First World War, especially Wilfred Owen, for whom he felt great sympathy.

His English teacher was a man called Mr A.J. Canavan. He was an Irishman, a graduate of Trinity College, Dublin, and an enthusiast for the works of W.B. Yeats and Flann O'Brien. He said of Sam, "You know what makes teaching worthwhile? I'll tell you: it's when you get one pupil – just one is enough – who really responds to what you are trying to teach. Sam has been mine. He made it all worthwhile."

Mr A.J. Canavan developed a respiratory complaint and died at the age of fifty-six. He lived to hear, though, that Sam won his place to study English at Durham, and that gave him great pleasure. In his will, he left the pick of his library to Sam, who selected thirty books from his collection and took them with him to university. In each of these books he wrote, *This book belonged to a great man, Mr A.J. Canavan.*

Before he went to Durham, Sam's parents bought him two pairs of corduroy trousers, an Aran sweater, and a suit of thornproof tweed. This was in 1984, when people still wore suits and, for that matter, corduroy trousers. Sam did not particularly like jeans, anyway, although that was the uniform of most students by then. He rather hoped that he might look a bit like Dylan Thomas in his corduroy trousers, his old tweed jacket, and a wide tie he had bought at a church bazaar.

"Quite the literary gent," said his father. "Good for you, Sam."

They drove Sam to Durham and dropped him off at his university hostel. Sam's father helped him carry his possessions up to the study bedroom that was to be his home, while his mother went off to buy him some fruit and packets of biscuits. "You don't know what the food will be like," she said. "Best to be safe."

"It'll be fine, Mum," Sam assured her. She fussed so

much, but then she was his mother, and that was what mothers did. They fussed. He went on to remind her about the arrangements. It had all been spelled out in the leaflet they had sent him. "They provide two meals a day. That's what we pay for. All I have to do is get my own lunch."

"Don't forget to do that," she said. "You have to have regular meals. It's really important."

"For the brain," said his father, smiling.

He said goodbye to them and waved as their car drove away. He saw his mother turn in the passenger seat of the car and blow him a kiss. She had been crying just before they left, the tears running freely down her cheeks, her mascara smudged like ink in the rain. Then they were gone, and he turned to go back inside to begin the next three years of his life. He felt a sudden rush of excitement. This was the end of a long childhood. This was the beginning of his own adult life. This was the start of an adventure.

He drew in his breath. He felt almost dizzy with excitement. It was a feeling of extraordinary richness – of exhilaration, really. He could start to make decisions.

For the first six months of his university career, Sam lived in the student hostel to which he had been assigned on first arrival in Durham. But then he was asked by a young woman in his Victorian literature class whether he would like a place in the student flat in which she and three other friends lived. This was in a Victorian terrace and was larger than most places of that sort, having been formed by the knocking together of two modest cottages. This meant that there were five bedrooms, as well as a sitting room. There was a postage-stamp-sized garden at the back, looking down towards the river.

His friend was called Janie, and she came from Newcastle. The other students were Kate, who was studying music; Thomas, who was a mathematician; and Ben, who was studying philosophy and economics. "We get on well," said Janie. "You'll like it."

He hesitated. He was not sure what lay behind Janie's invitation. He looked at her enquiringly.

It was if she knew. "You may be wondering why I'm asking you," she said.

He looked away, embarrassed. "No. Not really."

But she did know. "Yes, you were. You were wondering whether I fancied you."

He blushed. "I wasn't." And then added, "That's ridiculous."

"I do like you," she said. "I wouldn't have asked you if I didn't like you. That wouldn't make sense, would it?"

"I suppose not."

"But I'm not sitting here hoping that you and I will be an item. I promise you I'm not doing that."

He nodded. "Of course you aren't."

"Good," she said. "I wanted to make that clear. We all have our own rooms. It works best like that."

He grinned. "Of course, it does. Flatmates are . . . well, flatmates."

"So?"

He made up his mind. "Yes. Why not?" He had

made friends at university, but few close ones. To be part of a small group like this – even though he had yet to meet the others – seemed to him to be just what he was looking for.

He was the last in, and so he had the worst room – one with a small window and a view only of the neighbour's shed. It was sparsely furnished, with a rickety table, a chair, and a small wardrobe. He pinned up a poster above his bed, to cover the stains – somebody had thrown a cup of coffee at the wall. The poster was a picture of Edward Hopper's *Nighthawks*.

"That's so sad, that picture," remarked Janie. "Look at them. Urban alienation."

"I don't know," he said. "They don't look unhappy."

"Why that picture?" she asked.

He shrugged. "Because maybe that's the way I feel," he said.

"Detached? Is that how you feel?"

He shook his head. "No. I wouldn't say that. I think the people in that painting are waiting for something to happen. And that might be how I feel, I suppose."

She looked at him. "And do you know what you're waiting for?"

He said that he did not. Most people, he felt, had no real idea of what they wanted out of life.

"Love?" she said. And then added quickly, "Does that sound corny? I think it does."

"No, it's not corny. It's true."

"Something can be both corny *and* true," she said. She gave him an intense look. "Don't leave it too late."

"Leave what?"

"Love. Don't leave it too late."

He laughed. "But I'm nineteen – same as you. We both have plenty of time."

"Maybe. Maybe not."

He was not sure how you fell in love. He wanted it to happen to him, but he had not experienced it yet. There had been nobody. He had been ready for it to happen, but it simply had not. He had thought, when he read Lawrence, that he might learn something there. Lawrence's characters were passionate; they felt things deeply. He tried to cultivate that ability in himself, but it did not seem to work. There was an earthy current, it seemed, that Lawrence seemed able to tap into; he had no feeling for that at all. He would never succeed in being Lawrentian.

But then it happened to him, and it happened in a way that he had not anticipated. He walked past Ben in the kitchen one evening – Ben was at the stove, and Sam wanted to retrieve something from the fridge. He passed him and their arms touched. He gave a start.

"Not much room," said Ben. "Sorry."

He felt as if he had touched a live electric wire. He looked at Ben and swallowed hard. This was not the way he had imagined it would be, but then everybody said that love caught you unawares, and that you could never tell under what guise it would come to you.

Impulsively, he said, "Do you like this place?"

Ben frowned. He gave Sam a quizzical look. "Where? Here? The flat? Durham? The world?"

"Any of the above," said Sam, and laughed.

But Ben had found the question interesting. He said, "I thought it would be different, somehow. I thought that when I got to university, everything would be clear. But it wasn't. It was the opposite, really."

Sam waited for him to explain. Ben looked into the pot on top of the stove. He was heating tomato soup, taken from a can.

"What I found," Ben continued, "was that instead of being simpler, everything became more complicated."

"But isn't that how life is?"

"I suppose so." Ben shrugged. "It's just that I hadn't expected it to be that way."

They stood in silence for a few moments. Then Ben said, "Have you ever been skydiving? I have, you know."

Sam was surprised. It had never occurred to him that anybody he knew would go skydiving. Why would they? He said, "You haven't, have you? Really? From an actual plane?"

"That's the way you do it," said Ben. "They take you up, and then you jump out. Not with a line attached. You count the seconds and then you pull the ripcord."

Sam rolled his eyes. "I can't imagine . . ."

"No, you can't. Because it's like nothing else."

Sam looked at him. Why had this happened? And would it last? It could not. It could not, because . . . Because it was not how he had planned things to be – in so far as he had planned anything; and because it was not going to work. Ben liked him – he considered him a friend, he imagined, but that was all there was to it.

He was seeing a girl called Anne – Sam had seen them together, and she came to the flat on occasions. They ate soup together, and she sometimes left chocolate chip cookies that she brought in a tin. Was she a skydiver too?

He left the kitchen and returned to his room. He felt ashamed of himself. They said there was nothing wrong with feeling like that – and how could there be, if that was the way you felt? What was wrong with finding that somebody else made sense of the world for you? What was wrong with thinking that somebody else was that significant? Nothing, he thought, and yet it was not to be, just as it was not to be for anybody who found love unreciprocated, unreturned. It was just the way things were. You couldn't have everything you wanted in this life: there were plenty of people who loved the wrong person, who loved somebody unattainable because the other person was involved with somebody else, or who would not, could not, notice them.

He sat at his desk. There was a book in front of him; he had been reading it before he went through to the kitchen. It was one of the books he had inherited from Mr A.J. Canavan, and he opened it now. It was a commentary on Shakespeare's sonnets, and he realised now that this is how Shakespeare felt. He had never understood that before; now he did. This is what the sonnets were about: a moment or two in a kitchen, a conversation about something that had nothing to do with anything; a feeling that the world was incomplete and would forever be incomplete, because of separation from somebody you just wanted to be with since you liked the way they looked at things, or what they said, or because they made you feel at one with whatever it was in the world that we needed to feel at one with. All of that. And Shakespeare had left us all those lines of pain and regret and beauty. He had left them there, to be misinterpreted by just about everybody, but to be understood by those who felt as he did about this, whatever *this* was.

Three years was a much shorter time than he had imagined it would be. In the week before their graduation, Sam and Janie went for an Indian meal together. They were more or less alone in the restaurant, because it was a warm summer evening and people wanted to be outside. From where they sat, they could see the sky outside, and it was almost without colour, so pale in its blueness, and so sad, said Janie. He asked, "But how can the sky be sad? The sky is just . . . just air."

Janie said, "We project our feelings onto the things around us. A landscape is sad or threatening or even happy because that's how we happen to feel when we look at it. That's pretty elementary."

He looked at her and smiled. "Pretty elementary?"

"Yes. You don't need a degree to grasp that."

"Yes, but that's what we're about to get. A degree from this –" he gestured out into the street – "from this ancient university."

"Well, not so ancient," she corrected him, "unless you think of all those monks." She paused. "It could have been much earlier, of course. I suppose you know that. It could have been much earlier if Oxford and Cambridge hadn't deliberately stopped it in the sixteen hundreds."

"Ignore them," said Sam.

"I do."

She looked at him across the table. "And now, we go our separate ways. All of us."

He nodded. "Work. The world. Reality."

"Are you looking forward to it?" she asked.

Sam hesitated before replying. "I'll miss this place. Friends . . . I'll miss my friends."

"You'll make new ones. And it's not as if we're going off to different planets."

He said that she was right, but he added that in practice he thought it would be hard to stay in touch with everybody. It always was – in spite of best intentions.

"Best intentions," she mused. Then she looked at him and said, "Will you see Ben, do you think?"

He was casual. "Perhaps. He's not sure where he's going to be, of course. He was talking about going to McGill in Quebec for a master's."

She looked thoughtful. "I like Ben a lot. I didn't when he first moved in, you know. I thought he didn't like me all that much."

Sam assured her that she was wrong. Ben definitely liked her.

"I know that," she said. "It's just that he's one of these people whom everybody likes because he's good-looking and funny and . . . well, you know how it is."

She stopped. Sam thought about what she had said: *you know how it is*. What did that mean?

"I like him," he said.

She was watching him. "I know."

"But . . ." He shrugged.

She said, "I know, Sam. Yes."

He held her gaze. Then she said, "Is it that hard? Is it?"

He nodded. "Very hard. Sometimes. And then at other times, no, not at all."

"Which I suppose is what life is going to be like from now on – for all of us."

He smiled at her. "I like you too, of course. Even though you sometimes don't wash up all the plates you use. And you definitely use my milk from the fridge, without asking – I've seen you, you know. You think I haven't, but I have. I notice these things, Janie."

She made a show of mock contrition. "But have you forgiven me?"

"Of course I have."

Two

Brock Maxwell was a successful author. At the age of fifty-four, he was one of the bestselling writers in the country and was published in eighteen languages. Three films had been made of his work, starring actors whom the public went to see irrespective of the film's plot, or lack of it. His memoir, *The View from the Top*, was the most extensively borrowed biography in the public library system, and it was followed by a book of essays, entitled *You're It*. He was often seen on television discussing matters of the day, on which he inevitably had firm views.

It was an open secret amongst publishers that Maxwell could not write.

"He's virtually illiterate," his principal publisher said to a friend. "Tell it not in Gath, and publish it not in the streets of Ashkelon, but Maxwell can't write for toffee."

"And yet," pointed out the friend, "and yet, you publish him, don't you? And people buy his books by the bucketload. What's the secret?"

The publisher grinned. Lowering his voice, although they were quite alone, he confided, "Look, he came to us out of the blue. Slush pile stuff. I've always made it a rule – rule number one, I call it – that you look at everything that comes in. And I mean, everything. Why? I'll tell you. Because there are a lot of stories – and few of them apocryphal – about how people turned down major bestsellers. Everybody has one of those stories. Somebody rejects something that goes next door and, wham, hits the jackpot. Sorry, Mr Homer, your Trojan War story just won't sell. Yes, yes, the wooden horse is interesting, but that's not what readers these days are looking for. And look, Mr Hemingway, I think you can write – I'm not saying you can't write – but nobody wants to read about deep sea fishing these days. And as for you Mrs Christie – a body in the *library*, you say. Come on! Get real.

"Anyway, we had somebody going through the

slush pile of unsolicited manuscripts – an unpaid intern, actually. She was a niece of one of our board members, and she was marking time before going on to something else. I think she was getting married to the son of some landed chap in the Cotswolds. In other words, she was about to *disappear*, but she wanted to have something on her CV. So, her job was to make tea and smile at everybody and go through the slush pile to see if there was anything in there that might need a second look by somebody who knew what they were doing. She liked it, she said. She said that it was an effort sometimes to tear herself away from some of the things she read. Ninety-nine point nine per cent of it was pure rubbish, but occasionally she stumbled on something readable.

"She told me about some of the things she read, and we had a good laugh. Some of them were outrageous – fantasies of one sort or another, by people one would obviously not want to meet. Others were unintelligible. Most needed no more than forty seconds before they could be discarded. So, if you came across a manuscript with the dedication *To the cats in my life*, you did not really have to spend much time reading any further. Nor did you have to bother too much with the romantic novels involving nurses and doctors. Those exist, you know. They exist in their hundreds. Or the sort of book that she mentioned to me one day – volume one of a proposed series, *Nudist Camp Romances*. I'm not making that up. Somebody actually submitted that.

"But she came to see me one morning and said that she had found something with a very exciting plot. 'It's not at all well written,' she said, 'but it's compelling. I don't know why – it's just a compelling story.'

"I took a look at it, and I had to agree. The writing was appalling – clearly the work of somebody who had been taught no grammar, but the ins and outs of the plot were riveting. We decided to call it in. I wrote to the author and asked him to drop in to see us.

"He turned up, and that was how I first met Brock Maxwell. He came to see me four days later, and that was how it all began.

"Would you like to know what he was like? All right. Arrogant. Really pleased with himself. He had made a modest success of a horse stud somewhere, and he thought he could repeat this elsewhere. In fact, he said to me, 'I've decided to move into literature.' Those were his exact words – I shall never forget them. I sat there, utterly astonished at his sheer nerve. But I had a feeling, you see, that this rubbish that he was writing would go down well with people who like rubbish, and there are an awful lot of those. Millions, in fact.

"So, we decided to publish that first novel of his. It was called *The Big Grab*, and it was about somebody who stole an airliner. That was the territory we were in. It transpired that it was an inside job, and the pilot was in on it. I suppose he had to be. Of course, every sentence needed to be rewritten – verbs added, and so on. We had a freelancer on our books, somebody who had spent years editing a *Letters to the Editor* column on a newspaper and who knew how to make rubbish intelligible. He did a good enough job, but then he went and died, and so we had to give the job of editing the next one to an in-house person. Fortunately, we had somebody who had been with us six years and was good with a blue pencil. An English graduate. He did the next one, and the one after that. He's on the fourth now.

"But let me tell you a bit about our friend Brock Maxwell. He's bought himself a house in the country. He mixes with the smartest company. He thinks he's the expert on everything. And all the time, he's completely ignorant, and he still can't write. All he does is invent his ridiculous stories and then write them in his irretrievably adolescent style. We do the rest – all of it. He makes a great deal of money and plays the *grand seigneur* as a result. And he treats people abominably. Our younger staff are terrified of him, as are junior booksellers. He makes people cry, you know. If anything is not exactly as he wants it to be, he sounds off and creates one heck of a stink.

"And yet, the readers love him. We go into reprints almost immediately, no matter how many copies we print. The public can't get enough of him, but then, the less said about the intelligence of the public, the better, I suppose. Does that sound condescending? I suppose it does. But it's true – it really is. We live in an age when people have been encouraged to be stupid. We've dumbed everything down more than anybody would have thought possible, but still there are further depths to be plumbed. Watch this space – just watch it."

Sam drove out from Oxford in a car he had hired for the day. He normally met Brock Maxwell in the office in London, but had, on occasion, taken proofs out to him at his house, or had a meeting there to discuss some queries that a copy editor had raised. He did not relish these meetings, because Brock Maxwell always seemed scornful of him in some indefinable way. He looks down on me, Sam thought. He doesn't like me.

On this occasion, he was taking a corrected draft for the author's approval. The manuscript had needed extensive rewriting – as it usually did – but Sam did not imagine that their meeting would take unduly long, as Brock Maxwell tended to accept his suggestions without demur. Whole pages could be rewritten – sometimes being changed out of all recognition – and simply approved with a cursory glance and a nod. He did not think that it would be any different this time.

Sam was now twenty-seven. He had been with the publishing firm since graduation, six years ago, and he enjoyed his job. He had progressed rapidly, as he had a good grasp of public tastes and a sound eye for editing. He found rewriting easy, and he felt proud of the way in which he could transform Maxwell's sloppy and ungrammatical prose – no more than ill-thought-out jottings, if one were to be brutally honest about it – into coherent prose.

He was happy. He had used an inheritance from an uncle to pay the deposit on a flat in Jericho, in the centre of Oxford, and he was able to do a lot of his work from home. He went into London twice a week, to show his face about the office, but his real work was done in his study, with its view of the canal and the tow-path that ran alongside it. The only drawback was a small pub at the end of his street. This attracted a particularly noisy breed of undergraduate, and they sometimes woke him up at midnight with their inconsiderate shouting. But that was a small thing: what counted was that Sam liked the place he lived in, enjoyed the work that he did, and had a circle of good friends in the area. One of these was Janie, who had ended up living just around the corner from him. They met three or four times a week and shared a meal, or coffee, or simply each other's company. He might be in love with her, he thought. Just. It was possible. He dreamed of her a lot; only the previous night he had dreamed that they were playing tennis together, which they had never done in their waking hours. Did exercise in your sleep count? he wondered – and smiled at the absurdity of the question.

He thought that he would invite Janie to move in with him, now that the lease on her minuscule flat had come to an end. They had lived together before – and he thought they might do so again. She had hinted at it – or, at least, he had thought she was hinting at – and it made sense to split bills in this life, just as they had done when they were students in Durham. He thought of them – his flatmates of those days – and wondered what the others were doing: Ben, for instance. And for a few moments he imagined his friend tumbling through the sky, his arms spread wide, briefly a bird in flight.

Now, parking the car under one of the trees that lined Brock Maxwell's drive, he saw Beth Maxwell – "Long-suffering woman," their sales director had sighed – looking out of a window. And then she opened the front door, smiled weakly, as if to sympathise with him, before showing him into the drawing room. Brock Maxwell was sitting on a sofa, holding a newspaper, which he tossed down on the floor when Sam came in. He glanced at his watch. Even from a distance, Sam could tell that it was an expensive one.

"You're late," said the great man. "I've been waiting."

Sam looked down at his own watch. They had agreed that he would arrive at ten thirty. It was now ten thirty-four.

"I'm very sorry, sir." The "sir" slipped out; he was back at school for a moment, although this was no Mr A.J. Canavan, who disapproved of rudeness, who never spoke harshly or unkindly.

The apology was ignored. "You've done the final chapters?"

Sam nodded. "What I've done is to—"

He was not allowed to finish. "Sit down. Here. Next to me. Coffee?" It was a series of commands – even the last one, which was nominally a question.

"That would be nice. Thank you."

He sat down on the sofa and extracted the sheaf of papers that constituted the final chapters of *Call at Midnight*.

"I must say that the action is very gripping," Sam began. And it was, he thought, although the writing was appalling, the characterisation one-dimensional, and the sub-text of selfishness repulsive.

"Naturally," said the great man. "That's what they expect."

The readers were always "they"; Sam had noticed that before. It was a universe of "I" and "they".

"And they get it," he muttered.

The great man gave him a sideways glance. "Let's get on with it," he said.

Sam watched as Brock Maxwell shuffled through the pages, hardly bothering to read the numerous sections that had been entirely re-written.

"You've been busy, young man."

Sam smiled. "I do my best. And I know that you don't mind my being . . . proactive."

Brock Maxwell said nothing. He turned over a page.

Then Sam said something that was to change everything. He said it without any thought as to the consequences; he did not mean it, really. It was another of those instances where something slips out – just as the "sir" had slipped out earlier on. "Don't worry: I don't think anybody will ever discover I've written half of this."

He laughed as he spoke, but the great man did not. The great man froze.

"What did you say?" Brock Maxwell's tone was icy.

"I was only joking."

There was complete silence. Then, very quietly, the great man flicked through the last of the pages and handed them to Sam. "Right," he said.

Sam had realised his mistake. "I'm sorry," he said. "I didn't mean—"

Brock Maxwell cut him short. "That's fine," he said. "Send me a proof once you have one."

"There'll be time for another meeting," Sam said. "If there's anything that needs sorting out. We're ahead of schedule here."

The great man stood up. He ignored what Sam had just said.

"My wife will show you out."

And with that he left the room. Sam looked glumly at the manuscript in his hand.

Three days later, the publisher called Sam into his office. He looked grave.

"Look, Sam," he said, "this is very awkward. You said something to Brock Maxwell."

Sam felt his knees go weak. "May I sit down?'

"Of course."

"I didn't mean to offend him," he said. "I really didn't."

"I'm sure you didn't," said the publisher. "I know you well enough to be aware of that." He shook his head. "Perhaps you should tell me what you *did* say."

Sam explained. The publisher listened and, when Sam had finished, he groaned. "I can just imagine it," he said.

"I apologised," said Sam. "I said sorry straight away."

The publisher made a despairing gesture. "He's put a gun to our head."

Sam closed his eyes.

"Yes," said the publisher. "He says either you go or he does. He says that if you're still on the staff in a month's time, his next title goes to somebody else. The works. Paperback. Audio. Everything." He paused. "And you know what that means, of course. Roughly twenty-three per cent of our net annual profit."

Sam stared down at his feet.

"I've spoken to the chairman," the publisher went on. "He's prepared to stand by you, as am I. However, we have come up with what we might call a compromise solution. Would you like to hear about it?"

Sam nodded.

"If you resign," the publisher continued, "I'll do everything I can to get you another job. In fact, I have already lined up something for you to consider. But, more than that, we've worked out a financial package. You'll get an *ex gratia* payment of a full year's salary. I've spoken to the lawyers, and they point out that if we were to dismiss you, and you took us to a tribunal, the whole business would cost us a lot of money anyway. So, this really should save everybody something in the long run."

The publisher stopped. He looked at his hands, folded together before him on the desk. "I feel wretched about this," he said. "But there are other jobs on the line, you know. If we lost Maxwell, we'd have to get rid of three members of staff, including Molly, whose husband, as you may know, is far from well."

Sam raised a hand to stop him. "I accept," he said. "It's my fault."

"I feel so embarrassed," said the publisher.

"You mustn't," said Sam. "You've been very decent about it."

"I can't stand that man," said the publisher.

"I suspect you're not alone."

They both laughed.

"And the job you mentioned?"

"Ah, yes. My brother-in-law, Chris, as you may know, runs a medium-sized literary festival in the Cotswolds. He's in charge, but they need an assistant director. The salary's not bad, and the work is very interesting. You could combine it with freelance editorial work. You'd be better off in the long run."

Sam did not have to think much about this. "Thank you," he said.

The publisher was relieved that what he had feared would be a very painful meeting had gone so smoothly. "That man," he said, shaking his head. "I wish that Nemesis would pick him up on her radar. One, two, three . . . bang."

Three

"Poor Sam," said Janie. "Poor you. Poor, poor Sammy."

They were having dinner together, and Sam had cooked a beef stroganoff. Janie's expression of sympathy came after Sam had told her that one of the authors appearing at the festival was to be none other than Brock Maxwell. But, more immediately, he had to ask her not to call him Sammy.

"Look," he said, "you can call me Samuel – although nobody else does. You can call me You, or you can use my surname . . ."

"I can't call you Wallace."

"It's my surname." And, he remembered, it was what Mr A.J. Canavan called him. "Don't forget Eliot, Wallace. Go back to the *Four Quartets*. Luxuriate in the language . . ."

"It may be your surname, but you're not Wallace to me." She paused. "It makes me think of Wallis Simpson."

"Well, don't call me *Sammy*, all right?"

She bowed her head in acceptance. "This stroganoff is fantastic. But are you going to have to deal with him?"

Sam shook his head. "No. William is."

William was the publicity director of the literary festival.

"He might have forgotten by now," said Janie. "How many years ago was it?"

"Four," said Sam.

"Well, a lot has happened since then. I suspect he'll have forgotten who you are. Characters like that only remember the people they meet if they're important. No disrespect to you, of course . . ."

Sam said that she was probably right. "But this is the interesting bit," he said. "You won't believe this."

She waited.

"William had planned a special event," Sam went on. "He's having a big marquee *Mastermind*-type event. A quiz for celebrities. They get up on stage and are asked general knowledge questions and a special subject. The usual sort of thing. We've got four people signed up for it, including that famous footballer who claims to have written a book. It was ghost-written, of course, but everybody's being polite and not mentioning that."

"And Brock Maxwell?"

"He agreed to participate, but . . ."

"He wants top billing?"

"No, he didn't say anything about that. What he wants is to see the questions in advance."

Janie gasped. "No!"

"Yes."

"What did William say? Did he tell him to get lost?"

Sam shook his head. "I was really surprised that William agreed. He said that it will make a real difference to the crowd that day, and that will have a knock-on effect on book sales – on everything, really. They'll come to hear the great Brock Maxwell."

"But that's so dishonest," protested Janie.

"That's what I told him," Sam said. "But he just smiled."

"That's all?"

"Yes. He just smiled."

"So, he's going to come across as being impressively well informed?" exclaimed Janie.

"That's very much in character," Sam said. "There's a massive ego there."

Janie looked thoughtful. "What are you going to do?"

Sam shrugged. "Nothing. It's William's event. I've told him I don't approve, but I can't throw my weight around."

Janie looked unhappy. "Sickening," she said.

Sam agreed. "Sometimes I think the world's a very flawed place," he said. "It's full of deception, of one sort or another. Falsity. Lies. Bullying behaviour."

"And boastfulness," added Janie.

"That too," said Sam.

They lapsed into silence. After they finished their meal, they turned on the television and watched an episode in a crime series. They knew the villain would get his just deserts – that always happened in the parallel world that was portrayed on screen, even if it only rarely happened in real life.

They noticed the effect of Brock Maxwell's appearance at the festival. Although they usually got better crowds on the third day of the festival – always a Saturday – on this occasion there were at least another two thousand people thronging into the grounds of the country park where the events took place. Sam was wary: he had no intention of bumping into Brock Maxwell, and so he asked one of his assistants to tell him when the great man arrived.

"Here now," the young man told him, just before lunch. "Big car – lots of fuss. He insisted on bringing the car into the grounds. What a . . ."

He did not complete the remark, just looked away. The volunteers who helped at the festival were all told not to be rude to the guests, whatever the provocation.

"It's all right," said Sam. "A commonly held opinion."

Shortly before the author *Mastermind* event was due to be held, Sam met William in the office tent.

"A big crowd, I see," Sam said. "Well done."

"Ten thousand pounds in ticket money," said William, smiling with pleasure. "How's that?"

"Not at all bad," said Sam.

William drew him aside. "I know you disapprove."

Sam said nothing.

"You do, don't you?" William persisted.

"Well," said Sam, "I think it's dishonest. He's deceiving his own fans. And we're letting him do it. That makes us . . ."

"Accomplices?" supplied William.

"In a word, yes."

William lowered his voice. "Actually, I have a score to settle with that man."

Sam stared at him. "With Maxwell?"

William looked about him. There was a general hustle and bustle in the tent, but nobody could overhear their conversation. "He humiliated me once," he said. "It was years ago. I was working in a large bookshop in Manchester. I was in charge of events. Maxwell came to do a talk and there were large crowds – really large crowds. We ran out of stock for the signing. I'd ordered plenty, but we hadn't anticipated quite as many people would come along to get a signed copy of his . . . of his rubbish. Anyway, they did. And then we ran out . . ."

Sam listened intently.

"When we ran out, Maxwell got hold of the microphone and announced to the whole shop that the organiser of the event – and he named me – was completely useless. He said, 'He calls himself a bookseller, but draw your own conclusions everyone.' And then he stormed off. My manager was furious – with me."

Sam shook his head. He was not surprised. "That's the way he treats people," he said. "No surprises there."

But he was surprised that William should so readily have fallen in with the author's outrageous insistence on seeing his quiz questions in advance.

But then William said, "Payback day today."

William took some papers from a file. "See these?" he said. "These are copies of the question sheets we gave to Maxwell. These are the questions he will be expecting and will have prepared the answers for." He held up a different set of sheets. "And these – these are the questions I'm going to give the quizmaster." He grinned. "Different, you see."

Sam gasped. "He doesn't know that?"

William was triumphant. "Of course not. He's going to go on stage thinking that he'll make a clean sweep and that everyone will be vastly impressed with the range of his knowledge. Big genius. Big genius. But –" he paused, savouring the moment – "but, in fact, he's going to get zero because he won't know any of the answers. His natural ignorance – which is fathomless, I believe – will be revealed."

William rolled his eyes with delight. He thrust a copy of each sheet into Sam's hand. "Watch from the wings. Watch it all unfold – every glorious moment of it."

Sam was silent. The event was now about to start, and one of the volunteers had brought the team of three authors, including Brock Maxwell, to the back of the tent. It had been planned that they would walk down the aisle acknowledging the applause that would greet their arrival. Brock Maxwell's fans would be especially excited, as some of them were already sneaking photographs of their hero.

Sam stood well back out of sight of the audience. From where he was, at the side of the stage, he was partly obscured from view even by the participants – although if Brock Maxwell turned and craned his neck, he might see him.

The quizmaster came on stage and began proceedings. When he introduced Brock Maxwell, the applause was thunderous.

The other two authors went first. They were asked a range of general knowledge questions, and then questions around a special subject they had chosen themselves. Some of the questions were intended to be humorous, and they brought laughter from the crowd. Between each author, a musician came on stage and entertained the crowd for five minutes or so. The audience enjoyed itself.

Then it was Brock Maxwell's turn. He stood behind the contestants' podium, confident and smirking. The quizmaster reached for his sheet of questions and posed the first question. "Who was the first person to climb Mount Everest?"

There was complete silence. Brock Maxwell frowned. He stared at the quizmaster. "Could you repeat that?" he asked.

"The question is: who was the first person to climb Mount Everest?" And then, "I take it you've heard of Mount Everest, Mr Maxwell?"

Brock Maxwell looked down at the floor. "Pass," he muttered.

The answer was given. "I would have accepted either Edmund Hillary or Tenzing Norgay," said the quizmaster.

The next question was asked: "Who wrote the novel *Brideshead Revisited*?"

The clock at the back of the stage ticked. The audience murmured.

"Somerset Maugham?"

"No. Somerset Maugham did not write *Brideshead Revisited*. Nor did you, I believe, Mr Maxwell!"

The audience loved the joke. Brock Maxwell smarted.

I am witnessing, thought Sam, a man's humiliation. That is what this is: a public humiliation. Then he said to himself, And it is exactly the same humiliation that he has inflicted on others. Exactly the same. Is this how it has to be?

Sam heard the voice of Mr A.J. Canavan. He was sure he heard him.

And that is the point at which he stepped forward onto the stage. The quizmaster looked at him with surprise. He knew, though, that Sam was the assistant director, and so he did not challenge him as Sam gave him the other sheet of questions – the one that Brock Maxwell had already seen.

"A bit of a mix-up," Sam whispered to the quizmaster, taking from him the sheet of unseen questions. "Here. These are the right ones."

The quizmaster shrugged. He had not been told of William's agreement with Brock Maxwell. "Administrative error," he announced to the audience, who laughed appreciatively.

From the podium, Brock Maxwell watched Sam. His expression was impassive. The event continued.

"Now, Mr Maxwell," the quizmaster continued, "after that brief mix-up: With which city in India was the production of jute particularly associated?"

Brock Maxwell smiled. "Calcutta. Or Kolkata, as it

now is. It changed its name in 2001, to match the Bengali pronunciation."

"That's impressive," said the quizmaster.

The audience applauded.

And then, "Here's a tough one: can you name the three astronauts who took part in the Apollo 13 mission?"

Brock Maxwell put a hand to his brow, to give the impression of thinking. "I'll try," he said. "Let me see now: James Lovell, Fred Haise and . . . and . . ." The audience held its breath. "And Jack Swigert."

The quizmaster was impressed. "Absolutely," he exclaimed.

"James Lovell had already flown three missions," Brock Maxwell continued. "He had clocked up five hundred and seventy-two space flight hours before the mission began."

There was an audible intake of breath from the audience. Everybody was astonished. "He's brilliant," whispered a woman in the front row to her friend beside her. The friend nodded. "Amazing," she whispered back.

It was Brock Maxwell who sought out Sam afterwards. Sam had not intended to meet him, but the great man found him in the office tent. He drew him aside.

"I wanted to see you," he said. "We haven't seen one another for . . . for what? Five years?"

"Four," said Sam.

Brock Maxwell's gaze was unrelentless. "What happened back there?"

"A mix-up," said Sam.

"You saved me."

"Perhaps," said Sam.

Brock Maxwell was silent. He looked up at the roof of the tent. Then he lowered his eyes. "I think I might owe you an apology," he said.

Sam hesitated. "You might also owe an apology to William, you know."

It was a few moments before this drew a response. Then, "Perhaps. But you . . . Will you forgive me now?"

"I already had," said Sam.

Janie cooked dinner that night. She said to Sam, "You're tired."

He said, "It's been a long day."

"Of course. And tomorrow's a big day too."

"Yes. But it's all going well. Really well."

They looked at one another and smiled. It was.